The Testimony of Mr. Bones

Stories by Olive Ghiselin

The Testimony of Mr. Bones

The Testimony of Mr. Bones

Stories by Olive Ghiselin

TEAL PRESS
Santa Fe, New Mexico

These stories appeared originally in the following publications:

Quarterly West: "Signora Grigia"; *Western Humanities Review:* "The Poet and the Fishwife", "A Place With No Blackbirds on the Lawn", "The Loiterer", "Forsaking All Others", "Carl Gustav Larus", "The Spacious World of Aunt Louise"; *Michigan Quarterly Review:* "The Dampened Butterfly", "Mary Manfield's Garden", "Mrs. Homo Sapiens", "The Testimony of Mr. Bones"; *Utah Holiday:* "The World of Borg", "At Dan's Place", "A Little Night Music", "Grandpa Pigeon", "The Convergence of Gerda"; *The Sewanee Review:* "The Smiling Angel". The story, "Ah Love, Remember Felis" appeared in *Western Humanities Review* and appears in the anthology, *Best of the West* published by Peregrine Smith Books, 1989.

Copyright © 1989 by Olive Ghiselin
First Edition
All rights reserved
Printed in the United States of America

Library of Congress Cataloging-in-Publication Data
Ghiselin, Olive.
    The testimony of Mr. Bones : stories/by Olive Ghiselin. — 1st ed.
      p.   cm.
    ISBN 0-913793-11-6 : $10.00
    I. Title.
PS3557.H55T47   1989   89-20215
813'.54—dc20   CIP

Book Design by Robert Jebb
The watercolor appearing on the cover was created by artist Robert Harvey especially for this first edition
Typographics by Copygraphics, Inc., Santa Fe, New Mexico

Teal Press books are Smyth sewn for durability and printed on acid-free paper for longevity.

Teal Press
P.O. Box 4098
Santa Fe, New Mexico 87502-4098

For Brewster

Contents

The Testimony of Mr. Bones

Stories by Olive Ghiselin

Signora Grigia

"But Amalfi is such a dull little town," he said, in that soft gently ironic tone that is such an advantage to him in the classroom or at dinner parties. It meant what a little fool you are to make such a choice. It meant reconsider your taste. It meant you are much too pretty not to know better, and I challenge you to try. That voice had charmed me once, had almost persuaded me that it spoke gospel, though the words were so ungodly and so worldly. It almost persuaded me that I should enter its elaborate world.

I lacked the knowledge and the words to refute him then. Even today I can only say, "But I like Amalfi," offering the validity of feeling against the demonstration of error. Dull as it is, compared to Rome, or Milan, or Florence. Or Naples up the road a little way, where one is warned never to leave one's car or turn one's back, and beggars beset one persistent as gnats at evening. Or Positano, even closer, full of arty-crafty shops and lolling tourists. So I returned to it.

Amalfi certainly isn't where the action is. Not now. Once galleys and galleons of all the seas met here, and their mingling must often have been rude or violent. Even today neighboring Atrani keeps its big bell chained to prevent Amalfi from stealing it again. My friend could have read about this in the guide book the time he stopped, en route to somewhere else.

Several times a day buses arrive and tourists debouch, swinging cameras and bags. They stand in the little Piazza looking up at the Cathedral of San Andrea, who is the patron saint of fishermen. He lifts his hand in blessing from the black and white facade. Then they climb the many steps, past the oriental-looking tower, and inspect the Baroque interior. They visit the pretty Cloisters of Paradise, filled with sarcophagi on which Italians avid for immortality have scratched their names. Then

11

they descend and take pictures of the fountain whose stone woman spouts water from her breasts. If a white bull is being led up the street they snap a picture of that, or of the fishmonger holding up a long fish like a strip of aluminum foil. They buy a few things in the shops, and leave. The Piazza is given back to the natives marketing and gossiping. After sundown even the loungers go away. A woman may hurry through carrying a pot of red coals. At night the cats have the cobblestones almost to themselves. One can hear the fountain, and occasional hurrying footsteps in high heels or heavy boots. At the top of the hill, where the road and the town end, the rats probably come out to collect garbage in the deep gully. I have seen only one or two at noon.

The stout woman with greying hair and a grey sweater, who lives beside the steps to the Cathedral in an apartment on the second floor (it would be the third floor in America) closes her shutters at evening. Early in the morning she opens them and looks out. She is dressed in the grey sweater, but her hair is still uncombed. She runs her fingers through it, scratching and combing. Her face is blurred with sleep, but her black eyes are awake, darting at everything. She inspects the pots of blood-red geraniums on the sill, pulling off dead blossoms, and waters them. Later she reappears, her hair combed back in a bun. All day she comes to the window, her big breasts heavy on her folded arms, and watches. Occasionally someone calls up to her, a few words. She answers briefly. Sometime during the morning she lets down a basket to the shopkeeper, who fills it with vegetables, eggs, bread, three small fish. She draws it up and disappears for awhile.

Signora Grigia, I call her. After high noon her apartment is in shade. I see her sometimes moving in the dusk of her room lit by a small hanging electric bulb. But usually she keeps the shutters closed when the light is lit. Late at night she sometimes opens them again. I can see her unmoving bulk at the window.

What is it like, to live always in this choice box seat above the cobbled stage of Amalfi? Why does she seem never to leave it, for intermission, to mingle with others, to stretch her legs or drink a glass of something at a bar? Has she had enough of life already, been sufficiently jostled or flirted with, heard all possible comments about the success or failure of the production? Perhaps. Perhaps she is waiting for a fifth act that is never presented. Or waiting for someone to come.

She might have seen my friend the day he came to Amalfi and stood looking up at San Andrea for a minute. She would not remember him. He would not have noticed her. I use her ample flesh to defend the town against his allegation of its dullness. But it hardly needs defense. Its history has been written. I really use her to defend myself: There is life everywhere, even in this village, even in me.

A long while ago she was slim and lively. She was maid to a family who lived in a big house among the terraced lemon trees. It was a happy time for her. Her legs never tired as she ran up and down the hillsides. There were only two in the house, old people. When she had done the chores she was free to meet her lover, to walk in the scented woods above or by the moaning sea below. The only thing lacking was lire, enough to marry on, to buy a farm or a business. Only that.

Time passed, and with it the old wife. The sunken leather face proved that life was not eternal. But still the girl restrained her lover's urgency, and stayed his roughly tender hands. He was growing restless laboring in another man's orchard. He talked of foreign fields of opportunity.

One morning the girl found the old widower speechless in his bed. While he lingered, his left arm useless, she cared for him. Neighbors said she was a rare jewel, good as a daughter to the drooling old man. Word came that a nephew was coming to take over, but he was delayed.

When the girl was washing her employer in his bed another morning, thinking perhaps of what time does to the body of a man, he looked up at her, speechless as usual. But his eyes were saying something. The right side of his mouth twitched upward. Then his hand grabbed hers, and carried it to his person, pressed it against the fleshy piece of him that was like the neck of a dead chicken, held it there, rubbing roughly while she tried to pull away. At last she slapped him across the face with the hand that held the bath sponge. He relaxed his grip and his eyes closed.

That day she did not feed him again. That night she opened the chest where his papers were stored, and old pictures of weddings and relatives, and his money. She took as much as she dared—not all, but enough. "This hand has earned it," she said, and closed the box. She stayed on until the nephew arrived, to find his uncle unwashed and about to expire, and with less money than he had hoped.

The girl did not tell her lover about her theft. She could not speak of the old man's lechery to justify herself. She had fought too long to preserve the image of her virture, to be stained at this point by vileness.

But her lover talked more and more of going away. He had a cousin in Detroit, where he would prosper. All that was lacking was the boat fare. She had lire enough for that. Often she counted them, pondering her dilemma. In all the world there was no one to ask. She walked up the steep streets past arched alleys that smelled of urine, looking at doorways decorated with old scrolls and flowers, at the remains of palaces with shields on their faces, at a facade with octopi, and centaurs, and the lusty head of a satyr. They told her nothing.

Finally, with a sudden girding of her courage, she went to tell the secret to her lover. In the darkness she ran lightly along the narrow terraces toward his hut. At the door she saw him standing with another woman. She watched them kiss and heard their silly laughter. Fury and the smell of lemon blossoms filled her body, and she turned and clasped a rough cypress trunk until her passion was controlled.

Walking away, rubbing her arms where the bark had dented them, she plotted. Her heritage from this coast is ancient. If quickness does not serve, one waits. She smiled when she met her lover next, and left him time for his devices, which she shadowed. The midnight when the pair walked along the high sea cliff she crept behind them. When they locked in a mindless embrace on the edge, she darted and they toppled, grasping at each other's footlessness for safety. She watched them fall and returned to her sleepless bed.

When the pair on the cliff edge fell, their bodies off balance in their giddy pleasure, and splashed into the sea, the woman went quickly under. But the man survived. He knew who had pushed and punished them—both by the touch of her strength and his knowledge of the rightness of it. On this coast where the trade of the known world had come for centuries, oriental justice had often flashed with the speed of a drawn knife. And who knows who one's ancestors are.

So her lover had returned to her, in the brave fury that covers submission, and she had faced him, and their guilts had mingled and merged in reconciliation and renewal. Their troth was sanctified by secrecy and blood.

When the cousin wrote that all was not well in Detroit in those days, there was no work and not even any wine, they stayed where they had always been. It might have been better if they had gone away, to have their child among strangers.

For the child was strange. She could not walk or talk, or clothe or feed herself. And everyone knew what this meant. It was a visitation. In a world where the evil eye glanced everywhere, one was schooled in rites of prevention of evil. But they had been careless—or worse. No one knew anything, of course. But there were whispered conjectures and condolences.

Perhaps the wind of rumor kept her indoors, as much as the need to care for her child, who grew and grew and always was the same. Her husband turned out no worse than many another, perhaps better than most. He worked hard and was faithful, and did not squander her strange dowry. He is dead now, but the fruit of their union still hangs unripe and blemished, and will not fall to release her. Is this what she thinks of as she watches the movements in the little Piazza below San Andrea's Cathedral? The bars of white and black must make anyone think of daytime and darkness, and of good and evil, and of other alternatives for choice. Does she sometimes climb the many steps, at evening, to sit in the rear of the Cathedral in the silence when no rituals are being performed? Or does she only look up at it from her window, forever outside?

I stare at her from my window in the San Andrea Hotel. I have wondered if she recognizes me, that I have come back again this year after an absence, looking almost the same, standing gazing at the Piazza as I did before. Why don't I go to Rome, where one sits for thirty minutes in a traffic jam by the Colosseum and is late for luncheon at Ranieri's. Or to operatic Milan, or pigeon-dunged old Genoa, or Florence where ghosts of the Medici with poison in their girdles still stalk beside the Arno, which flows the color of jade by day and Duccio black at night. Why not indeed.

Here the silent hills are full of purple crocuses in spring. All year the sea cliffs erode so slowly that the falling grains make no sound.

I think I must have a taste for dullness. Perhaps this makes me dull. I must store up a few bright sayings, quotations from lively people, in case I sit by my friend again at a dinner party. He will be freshly back from a nightclub in Madrid, or a museum in Paris, or lunch in a famous musty club in London. He will speak in that same soft voice, faintly ironic, aware of aberrations and peccadillos, appraising and amused. Not quite scornful, not quite condescending. Urbane. He feels free to be teasing because I was once his student. Besides, he really likes me. Once we almost more than liked each other. Almost, not quite. Because it was almost, there is no awkwardness between us. When we meet at that future dinner party he will say, "You're looking wonderful." And I will say, "So are you." There will be a moment of silence while we lift our wine glasses and put them down. "What are you doing these days?" he will ask, politely.

Perhaps I will tell him that I've been reading about San Andrea, who was crucified in Greece. His bones came strangely to Amalfi, and sweat a miraculous medicine, for what ailment I don't know. Perhaps it is for that ailment that is worst of all—acedia, indifference, the boredom of the soul. "Still harping on Amalfi," he will say, telling me that I am mad, but it is an amusing madness, nothing sinister. We will smile and take another sip of wine, and look at each other across an enormous distance.

The Poet and the Fishwife

Once there was a poet who married a fishwife. He thought she would be interested in the beauties and wonders of the deep. But all she could do was gut and scale and slice fish. So he left her for a mermaid with a beautiful voice and a shiny long tail.

The mermaid knew a lot about sea caverns and other mysteries, but she never told him much. It was all old stuff to her. Also, he couldn't keep up with her in the sea caverns, and out of the water she was inclined to sit combing her hair and singing the same old songs over and over. She wasn't one for innovation. Rhymed iambic tetrameter was fine by her. When he gently suggested that she might like to try approximate rhyme or free verse she said, "Why?" After all she was a classic type. Sirens don't think they can be improved upon. And she wasn't any more interested in what he was writing than his wife had been.

The poet got tired of shucking his own oysters and eating cold mackerel. And the mermaid smelled of seaweed. And anatomically she was put together rather strangely and the novelty of that wore off. So one day he went back to land. It is doubtful that the mermaid missed him. There were always more where he came from.

As he walked along the dock, he anticipated his homecoming. The little apartment would be warm and dry, delightful after the vast moistness of his sojourn at sea. His Penelope would be warm and welcoming, her blonde hair neatly coiled and pinned around a head that thought only of him, her nether parts properly arranged to be disarranged on a proper mattress. He whistled as he walked like any sailor returning home. He was almost a classic type himself. "Home is the sailor, home from the sea" — Well, hardly all that. For a minute he wondered at exactly what point the classic becomes the corny. Then he hurried on.

Like other returned travelers he was due for a surprise. The apartment house he had left was gone. He felt as baffled as if terra firma itself had disappeared. The sea is known for its fluctuations, but the earth should remain the solid earth. He looked to a neon sign for guidance. Tina's, it said. Tina's Seafood Grotto.

He looked inside. There were tables with red cloths and candles. Along the walls festoons of fish nets were hung with shells and glass balls. People were dining in a redolence of wine and oil and garlic. And at the counter by the side sat Tina, coiffed and smiling, counting out change to a portly gentleman who had obviously dined well.

"My God!" said the poet. "My wife!" But he hesitated, seeing his reflection dimly in the window pane. He did look a bit incult, covered with dried salt and wrinkles. There were mussel scratches on his hands and a scar where an eel had bit him. His beard was unfashionably long and had some flotsam in it.

With his unfailing feeling for the appropriate, he decided not to stage a reunion in this public place and found his way to the back door. "I want to speak to the proprietress," he said to a waiter in a white linen jacket.

"What for? There aren't any jobs for dishwashers."

The old arrogance of the man used to telling things to people pulled itself together. "Convey to her the message that a relative has returned and wants to speak with her."

The waiter went off with his tray of crabs, but he took his time. The poet looked around. The kitchen gleamed with enamel and steel. Two chefs stirred and broiled. A wonderful odor of sea food raised to a high level of perfection by some mysterious acts of adding and dividing and mingling pervaded the room. Greens and vegetables were being chopped, flagons and decanters were tipped, bread cubes were toasted.

His whole body was consumed with hunger to consume. His recent diet seemed barbaric in this civilized haven where raw fish were sliced and simmered and transmuted. How beautiful were herbs, and yeast, and oil. How magnificent was the mind of man, to do all this. "Cooking must be the ultimate creative art," he said to the nearest chef in a passionate outpouring of conviction.

"Fine words fry no fish," he replied, skillfully turning a pair of bass in a copper skillet and sprinkling over them something that smelled like a sunny hillside.

When Tina entered the kitchen they looked at each other. "So you're back," she said with the talent for expressing the obvious that had sometimes annoyed him.

"As you see."

"I see you look a bit down at heel. Are you hungry?" She always had a sense of the realities of life, you could say that for her.

"Yes."

"Give him the twenty franc dinner," she instructed a waiter, "and a half litre of white." She turned to the poet. "You can wash yourself in the men's room."

The poet ate slowly after gulping his soup. Tina had not given him the most expensive meal—but neither had she given him the cheapest. As a symbolic act, this was just. He was seated at a single table next to the kitchen. He could watch the diners sipping, savoring, gorging. They looked happy as porpoises. They paid their bills with no regrets. Tina had a good thing here. How had she managed it?

When the front door closed and was barred after the last exit, Tina came to his table with two glasses of marc. For the first time he felt really warm. As he waited for her after his meal he had prepared an answer to her forthright wifely question: Where have you been? He had formulated a structure of reasonable substance, expressed in a cadence that would pierce her soul. He would explain his temporary mad disaffection with his way of life, and his subsequent disenchantment with what he had so stupidly chosen. But now he had returned to stay forever with her, his first and only and most true love. But Tina's words were chilling. He felt like a customer who discovers that he has no money to pay his bill.

"What do you plan to do now?" she asked. The question was as sharp as the stroke with which she used to cut off the head of a mullet.

He looked away. "I don't know."

"Well, you can stay here overnight. You can sleep on the bench by the coat rack."

The narrow hard bench was a coffin to his expectations. He got up and walked around in the gloom of the single light hanging in the window. His misery cried out in its natural medium. The verses poured from him in an unpremeditated hemorrhage.

I should have never
Started to roam.

19

Why did I ever
Wander from home.
Why did I ever
Leave the dear shore.
I will regret it
For evermore.
I was a fool
And now I repent.
All my past sins
I sadly lament.

Next morning, when Tina brought him a cup of coffee and a left-over roll and said, "Well?" he repeated them to her, sadly, contritely, con molto sentimento.

A flick of calculation removed the glaze from her eye. "Hmm," she said, as if considering the freshness of a kilo of codfish. He waited on the hook. "If you want to stay around and read your rhymes to the customers for your board, you can. You can sleep in the back storeroom." So he stayed.

Tina's guess was right. "The Lament of the Vagabond" became as popular as the stuffed clams. Everyone liked it, roamers and non-roamers. Philosophers interpreted it in a larger context of universal sin. Women loved it. As time went on he added verses and elaborated them. He played around with assonance and dipods and spondees and terza rima. As his reputation grew he sometimes made comments on politics in heroic couplets. Occasionally in the salmon season he wrote sonnets on the beauty of spring. But his pièce de résistance was the Ballad, elemental as the chunks of bread on the table. He attempted to make a few emendations to the menu by adding words like sizzling to the mixed grill, and succulent to the lobster, and unctuous to the sole in sauce Mornay. But Tina said no. "Use plenty of butter and you don't need this onomatopoeia stuff."

One evening a publisher chanced to dine at the Grotto. "You have a nice talent," he said to the poet. One thing led to another and a volume of his verse was printed. It sold almost as well as the bouillabaisse.

On a night when the wind was howling over the sea and rattling the shutters like the end of the world, Tina let him into her apartment. Thereafter they were commensal.

Strolling on the quay every morning for exercise—it was not good for a lamenting poet to look too well-fed, Tina chided—he sometimes looked out to sea, which stretched as vast as an epic on the life of man. Once he had looked on those waters with an avid eye. That was before he got salt in it. He would stare for awhile, and then walk back to the Grotto for lunch. In the afternoon he took a nap, to be fresh for the evening. He almost never thought of the mermaid. She never thought of him at all. Tina remembered her often enough to keep the fire of creative cooking aflame.

A Place With No Blackbirds
on the Lawn

Why the Silbermans came to San Carlos Bay at all was strange enough. Why hadn't they gone to Miami or Palm Springs or Santa Barbara. It turned out that a travel agent had recommended the place as picturesque and inexpensive, and they hadn't been to Mexico before. When they arrived one January afternoon, Margaret and Daniel were on their balcony which adjoined that of the newcomers with only a wall between. The sounds of Mrs. Silberman's disapprobation were immediately audible from the little apartment.

For one thing Jaime, the cleaning man, was taking a siesta on one of the beds and was not very embarrassed to be found doing so. When he had been dismissed, the Silbermans stepped out on their balcony. Most new tenants paused to look into the depth of blue bay below them, and across the water to the steep island decorated with candelabra of cactus spears, and then to the jagged mass of the Montaña Encantada beyond. They said How beautiful! Or Gee, this is great! But when Mrs. S. had finished talking about Jaime, she went inside to poke around.

Thereafter the Silbermans didn't do any of the usual things. They didn't fish, nor swim, nor sunbathe, like the other retired vacationers. They were from Illinois, and perhaps it was enough just to be in a benign sunshine. But they took daily constitutionals, wearing dark glasses and carrying walking sticks convenient for knocking something out of the path. Mrs. S. had thick short legs curved slightly outward. "Achondroplasia," said Daniel in the same tone he used to identify a tunicate or an oystercatcher. Her grey hair lay in curled obedience under a net. "It would be afraid to move around," said Margaret. "She'd snip it off."

On their walks they did not lean down to collect shells, or pause to look at whales or birds, even the ever-circling seagulls. The gulls were another irritation to Mrs. S. When they sailed low above the cliff, she waved her arm at them, shooing. But they interpreted this to mean that she was throwing something to eat, and came in raucous numbers, jostling and darting. Margaret explained that they were useful scavengers and kept the beaches clean. "They're dirty," said Mrs. S. "Filthy." Her porch steps had been fouled. And it was impossible to get Jaime to clean adequately. Methodically he mopped the center of the tile floor but was blind to anything in corners. He refused to learn to make a bed properly. "Stupid," said Mrs. S.

The Silbermans walked daily to the little Fruteria for supplies. She held cauliflower up to a grim inspection, poked into pineapples, squeezed oranges. When there were chickens she held one up by the legs and peered inside, like a gynecologist looking for a tumor, Margaret thought. At the fish cleaning table, where tourists gave their superfluous catch to the beach boys to sell, she haggled, at a disadvantage from knowing no Spanish. But she could change pesos into dollars in her head.

In the late afternoon the Silbermans sat on their balcony and read the newspaper which was flown down from Tucson. There was always an inexplicable lack of news from Chicago unless there had been a blizzard. Even the description of weddings was unsatisfactory, though bizarre. "The Andersons were married in a cactus garden in the desert," she observed aloud.

"Who are the Andersons?" asked Mr. S.

"They live in Tucson. They got married by a ceremony they wrote themselves. Poetry sort of."

"Humn," said Mr. S.

"It won't last," she prophesied.

The morning there was no water in the pipes, only the newcomers were surprised. Margaret kept her thermos bottles filled. She took one next door to the Silbermans. Mrs. S. seemed less grateful for water than outraged at the lack of it. "We do a lot of aquabatics down here," said Margaret, but Mrs. S. went on talking. This never happened at the Hilton, even the Hilton at Tucson.

No. At the Hilton the chlorinated water always flowed, hot and cold. The ice cubes were pure and unending. The TV flicked on in color in an instant. Room Service did not say Mañana, Mañana. In the grounds there were only blackbirds, who felt handsome on an ordered lawn, and sparrows, who had no sense of caste and went everywhere.

"This doesn't happen at the Hilton either," Margaret murmured to Daniel as they drank their coffee on the balcony. On the edge of the water an egret was standing, white and motionless, his shadow a small gleam beneath him. Then he walked forward on his long, black, fragile-as-steel legs, and the breeze ruffled his head feathers, and he uncurled his long neck, as elegant and disdainful as if the world were made for him. "How many worlds there are," she said. And Daniel, dumbly concerned with the satisfactions of his own, nodded.

Whatever the aberrations of the day, Margaret liked to go to bed with the assurance that the stars were in their accustomed places. Now I lay me down to sleep and pray the stars their place will keep. That night, looking up at them, she brushed away a mosquito and slapped another, and she and Daniel went indoors. "Does everything serve a purpose?" she asked. "Even mosquitoes?"

"We've been down that teleological path before. It has no ending."

"Don't use big words at me. I keep thinking everything ought to be of some use."

"You mean everything ought to be of some use to you. Now take mosquitoes. In their world, you are of use to them. You were put on this planet to feed them. It's against nature for you to come inside where they can't get you."

"They'll find a way," Margaret predicted.

"Actually we do their race a favor when we make window screens, because only the very smart ones will get through and survive."

"The idea of mosquitoes with a high IQ makes my blood run cold," said Margaret.

Next morning Margaret said, "What do you think Mrs. S.'s world is like?"

"It's full of outrages and indecencies and frustrations, to the end that her character will be strengthened and she will survive, while the rest of us will become extinct."

"She's strengthening Jaime's character by making him scrub the shower."

"There are always imponderables to confuse a pattern. Like we might get tired of her, or feel threatened, and push her off the cliff. We could, on the grounds that she has no redeeming social value."

"The seagulls would eat her," said Margaret.

"And the vultures."

"And the maggots."

"But not us. We're too civilized. Whatever that means," said Daniel.

"It means that we use big words," said Margaret.

Across the bay, the steep uninhabited island was a peninsula at low tide. One could walk over to it on a narrow passage way. There was nothing there but cactus and some shrubs and silence and a few pelicans roosting. People crossed over to explore the rock pools and were careful to come back before the tide turned. One evening a young couple paused on the shore and looked at the island. He had longish dark hair and a thick uncultivated beard, a type so fashionable that he was both generic and indistinguishable. The thin girl too was lost in the blue jeans and long blonde hair of her generation. She tied a bandana on her head as the man pointed. Coming up behind them Margaret heard her say, "There isn't any shelter."

The man said, "We don't need any. The sky's perfectly clear." She glanced back and saw them picking up their packs. When she got home, the two were crossing to the island. She knew how the stones tipped under their feet. They went slowly, balancing precariously under the heavy loads.

Such a jaunt took—what? Not courage. They were safer than on a highway. It took a taste for something different, a daring to be different, a willingness to be uncomfortable for the sake of something new. The stars would be magnificent out there. If one fell, unpredictable, unscheduled, it would be a happy omen. It was for her. She always hoped for one, a vagrant flash of unexpected light. The vagrants on the island might see one while she was sleeping.

Mrs. S. was also watching the pair. At the foot of the island they had trouble scaling the cliff. The man went first and then returned for the girl's pack and pulled her up. They stood resting and then climbed the short distance to the top and disappeared.

"They're probably not married," said Mrs. S. to Mr. S.

"Probably," he said.

"Or they'd go to a motel."

"Umn."

"Or they've got no money. Hippies." They went indoors.

Margaret stayed outside looking at the evening. Three Mexicans in a boat came and laid down a net in a big circle in the bay. The circumference was beaded with floats, like a string of perfect days in the wide turning year. The boat circled inside it several times. Then the men pulled in the silver net. But it was empty. Nothing at all. Nada. They chugged off into the darkening mouth of the bay. Two sanderlings flew fast and low over the water, following the cliff edge. How vulnerable they looked, little bits of porous bones and feathers and hot blood, going off into the darkness. Venus was a speck of light above the island. A little later she saw a wisp of smoke rising. The girl would be bending over, stirring something.

Sometime after midnight the wind gave a wail of warning and howled through the shutters. Then the rain started, quick and heavy. Margaret thought of the pair on the island. There were a few overhangs of rock. Perhaps they had put their sleeping bags under one. It must be very dark with the stars gone. She thought of the pelicans hunched into their waterproof feathers.

Next morning was clear but there was no smoke on the island. About noon, the couple came down to the passage way. It was still under water, but the tide was going out. Finally they took off their shoes and rolled up their levis and waded across, slowly because of the swirling over the loose stones. Margaret watched them reach the mainland and walk across the beach below her. They dropped their packs and sat down. Their pants legs were wet and they stretched their legs out in the sun. The girl was coughing.

Pretty soon Mrs. S. walked down her stairs and then along the path, swaying rather like a pelican. She was carrying a coffee can with both hands. She went to the young couple and said something. They looked at her and the man rose to his feet. Mrs. S. talked up at him and down at the girl. She emphasized her words with shakes of the head and handed the man the coffee can. Then she climbed the cliff.

Seeing Margaret and Daniel on the balcony as usual, she said, "The girl has a cold. I took them some chicken soup. She should have something decent to eat for once," and went indoors.

After a while Margaret said, "Do you have a big word for this phenomenon perhaps?"

Daniel said, "It's a gynecotropism. The compulsion of the female to feed anything that looks hungry. It doesn't really involve the brain. It's just a reflex mechanism. She sees an empty mouth and she pops a worm in."

"It doesn't mean anything?"

"Not a thing."

They sat watching the catspaws of afternoon running over the water, that seemed to be writing and erasing, writing and erasing, some simple frantic message.

Then Daniel said, "I'm hungry. Do I get any chicken soup?"

"Not unless you're getting a cold," said Margaret and went indoors to make sandwiches. She stopped with her knife lifted. "Predictability," she thought. "It's what I want and what I don't want." Her knife slowly sliced the cheese. "What if I should make a sandwich of two slices of cheddar and a slice of bread in between. I'll bet he'd have a name for it." But she didn't test him.

The Dampened Butterfly

The bricklayers slowly building the Camino del Sol Motel on the shore north of Mazatlan had as perfect a job as a man is likely to find, if he has to work. Because the motel was not to open for another year, the pace was pleasant. Of course there were reminders that it was some day to be finished. In one roofed-over room there had already been delivered fifty mattresses in heavy plastic covers. These were nice for the night watchman. The two night watchmen. One would be lonely, under the big stars, listening to night and other noises, and to the roosters who practiced crowing in the dark, and the burros mourning their losses, and the pounding sea. Two watchmen were companionable, and better. No passerby would carry off a mattress, probably, but tiles and bricks disappeared. Even sacks of cement.

It was a good job. One could go in the afternoon for a swim to wash away the plaster dust. The food vendor stopped his wagon in the road at lunch time from eleven until evening. One could smell him coming, the salsa very delicious. Someone could bicycle to the Mini Supermercado for beer. From the beach a peddler on horseback tossed up oranges. The workers stopped to eat them, throwing the peels down while they watched the tourists in their straw hats with paper flowers. This was one of the pleasures. The tourists paraded whenever the sun shone, which was usually. They walked their well-fed dogs. The dogs chased sea birds. The German shepherds guarding the hacienda walls barked themselves rigid with envy. Just now it was fashionable to prance along the beach like reined-in ponies. The bellies and bosoms rippled and bounced. Sometimes there were amazing beauties, like the blonde who almost flowed out of her almost bathing suit. Mama would die of shame to see it. Pedro missed her, being for the moment working. All afternoon they teased him. The blonde in the bikini never came again. She became instead a legend. Just as good for conversation, even for Pedro.

Some of the tourists stayed. The workers got to know them, walking on the beach, swimming, sunning themselves on the hot sand, their greased bodies cooking like a fillet of flounder. Muy loco. Even a cockroach prefers the cool shade.

One of those who stayed lived in a motel across the highway and several times a day he passed the Camino del Sol, where the bricks were slowly rising. Except that he was too tall he might have been a Mexican. His trousers were baggy. He wore huaraches with soles made of rubber tires, and a worker's sombrero. Sometimes he swam. Sometimes he sat on the sand not looking at anything. Sometimes he looked at everything. At the smashed rat on the highway, every day becoming flatter. The hermit crabs braiding their trail across the sand. The green iguanas in the palm trees, their crested length almost invisible against the leaves. The dolphins leaping beyond the line of waves.

Most often he looked at birds. At a hummingbird's nest with two bills like thorns sticking up. At the heavy-billed anis stalking crickets in the grass. At big yellow flycatchers with black masks, and the little cardenalitos that sit bright as drops of God's blood on the tops of bushes. This they heard about when the man talked to people on the beach. He usually carried binoculars, and people would say, "Bird watcher, huh?" Sometimes he would answer Yes or No and look annoyed. Other times he would have long conversations. Hernando could listen to English very well. He had lived in the San Joaquin Valley.

But the man seemed to like the sea birds best. He would sit a long time looking at the pelicans gliding above the lift of the waves. The great blue herons flapping to and from Deer Island. The frigate birds gathered like a dazzle of gnats over the island at sunset. Terns darting and falling. Willets feeding in the sand.

Even fish jumping interested him, though he never went fishing. When a sportsman left his catch gaping on the shore and walked away, the man put it back in the water with a frown. One night a large seal washed up on the beach, its skin very tight. All day people stopped to stare. A woman whose buttocks were sunburned through her lace bathing suit said, "He's an ugly beast isn't he."

The man said courteously, "You would be too, Madame, if you'd been dead three days." That was really when the workers started no-

30

ticing him.

They always called him El Hombre, never El Señor. He walked with a long stride, his arms swinging. The workers wondered what he did for a living. He had not enough paunch for a banker or a politician. His hair was not neat like a business man's generally. For a worker he had not enough muscles. Except for his car and binoculars he gave no signs of wealth, not even a wrist watch. He was not quite old enough to be a retired person like most of the tourists. Maybe he was a journalist, but he did not sit in bars or go about with a notebook asking questions. He could be a scientist, except that he did not kill things and put them in bottles. One morning he came from the beach carrying a sea snake dangling from a stick. He had found it dead on the shore. He held it up for the workers to see. Serpiente, they agreed. Later he took it to the Estacion de Biologia at Playa Norte where everyone was very happy and excited to see it, and the scientists put it in a bottle. So the Manager of the motel reported. It was only a small snake. Finally the workers considered that El Hombre might be a taxi driver on vacation. He drives as if he hates the bumps in the road, like a taxi driver at carnival. Reckless, they said.

Reckless too in a different way. At night he walked alone on the beach beyond where the lights of the motels stopped. The watchmen would see him. Didn't he know why the walls were topped with teeth of broken glass, why the dogs barked at night, why a light burned at doorways after sunset? The policemen patrolling the shore walked in pairs, not only for loneliness. Other things than swollen seals were found on the beach. The circling vultures knew. Smart birds, the vultures. Ugly, but smart.

The workers made jokes about El Hombre. Maybe they should use this opportunity. No day comes again. A wallet would be useful. Probably a money belt too. And the binoculars. Not at night! Si! Si! He looked at the stars. There were dark places. A quick lunge against a back with arms lifted. Very simple. As easy as laying bricks. Easier.

Next to the motel was a small house on the shore, and at the rear of this was the smaller house of the caretaker, Señora Valdez, and her six children. They were a good family. Everybody worked. Even the baby swept the patio, with a broom twice his length. Under the oleander bushes was a pen for the pig. Chickens roamed the yard looking for insects. One of the hens was tied by a leg to an oleander, and clucked to her small chicks that ran about her scratching feet. One noon when the workers were toasting tortillas on a piece of metal over a small fire near the little house, one of the chicks left the others and wandered into the road. At this instant El Hombre came along and with his sombrero shooed it from the path of a car. The next to the smallest Valdez boy came to catch it, but it swerved from him like a paper in the wind. With the speed of fall from grace it darted under the big iron gate of the hacienda next door. The boy lifted a stricken face to El Hombre. They both stood looking through the gate. The man made clucking noises. He sounded a little like a hen. Not enough. The workers laughed, forgetting the tortillas.

Then the man rang the bell at the gate, loudly. Soon the maid came. He made gestures. She unlocked the gate with a key. He crouched, holding his sombrero out. With a lunge he caught the chick. He bowed to the maid. He gave the peeping chick to the boy, who ran home too thankful to say thank you. But the workmen called "Gracias" as the man passed, and everybody smiled.

For the Valdez family it was no laughing matter. A chicken is a chicken. It will grow up, God willing, to become a meal or a mother. Where there are automobiles and rats it needs all the help it can get.

About other creatures one cannot be so sure.

The day El Hombre picked up the bright orange butterfly, the workers were just settling down for the siesta. A warm land wind was blowing white tassels on the wave caps, and blowing insects seaward from their dry fields where they are only eaten by birds and iguanas. At such times their wings become dampened. On the wet sand they die. The man saw the butterfly, like a moving bougainvillea blossom on the sand. He picked it up. It rested on his finger, orange in the sunlight, fluttering a little. After a few minutes he carried it to the edge of the beach and placed it on a bush. The drowsy men watched it awhile before it flew away.

"Idiotica," said Jose.

"Still, it was very pretty," said Hernando, who had a bougainvillea blossom in his shirt front. When they were washing their faces at the end of the day, someone wondered how the butterfly was faring. They told the watchmen about it, Pedro holding out his forefinger and fluttering the fingers of his other hand above it. They laughed and looked inland, into the distance of hills.

Next morning when the men came to work they paused as usual to see if the beach was as they had left it. Asleep under one of the thatched huts for the shelter of the tourists an unknown Mexican lay with his head on a bundle. Nothing unusual. Not until noon did someone tell the stranger to leave. He went into the bushes and came back, and sat leaning against the wall of the new motel. Later he bought a Coca Cola from the vendor, speaking to no one, and returned to the wall. When the two policemen came along the beach on their afternoon walk he went again into the bushes.

"Like a rat," said Jose.

At sundown he was still there. "A homeless rat," said Pablo, washing up to go home on the bus. "It is sad," he said, thinking of the warm smell of frijoles and mackerel on the fire. But he had earned them. The workers spoke of the stranger to the watchmen: Keep an eye on the tools.

Daylight was almost gone when the watchmen heard the sound of metal scraping. From the top balcony they looked down. The stranger was sitting on the sand sharpening a tire iron against a piece of concrete. They felt almost that they had been expecting this, like darkness after sunset.

"He's not going diving for oysters."

"For what then?"

Their skins itched a little with interest. The nights were long. Asleep much of the day, they missed sights for conversation. They got news secondhand. The first watchman had never forgiven himself for being inland when the hurricane struck, flooding the whole town and knocking coconuts from the broken trees. It was terrible to be there. It was misery to have missed it. The men listened until the grinding of the tire iron stopped. Then they watched the stars brighten and the islands disappear. They wondered what was going on in the city, where they could see the lights of the boulevard along the shore. They talked of buying a transistor radio some day. They took turns walking through the motel to the road and back.

It was late when El Hombre came down to the beach and strode northward into the night. They had not time to light cigarettes before they saw the stranger go from the shadow of the wall.

"The rat is getting hungry."

"Rats are always hungry."

"Even a rat must eat."

"Si."

"El Hombre is muy loco."

"Si."

"Still, he saved the Valdez' chicken."

"And he saved the dampened butterfly."

"Let us go." He picked up a hammer. The other picked up a short piece of pipe. They swung from the balcony, jumped to the beach, and ran northward, silent in the soft sand.

Beyond the place where the tourists with long curls and beards camp, the beach had been eaten away by high tides and the hurricane, leaving a small cliff. El Hombre stood below it, facing the sea. He would hear nothing but the swishing and pounding of the waves.

The watchmen had been right to hurry. When they saw the shape of the stranger crouching forward they did not wait. He turned, his right arm with the tire iron lifted. But the first watchman hit him above the ear with the hammer. The second did not need to use the pipe. The stranger tipped forward and collapsed on his face. Then he lifted shoulders, groaned a little, and crawled slowly toward the land. His body sagged like a half-smashed crab's.

The watchmen waited until El Hombre walked southward, following close to the white lace of the shore. Once he stopped, seeming to listen to the sad, harsh cry of a willet flying low over the water. At the motel, the men put down the hammer and the pipe. They lit cigarettes, looking at each other in the match light.

"Maybe the stranger meant no harm."

"You do not greet your grandmother with a tire iron."

"Maybe we will know tomorrow."

"Maybe the vultures will tell us."

A few days later El Hombre went away, going inland. Different people walked along the beach, less funny, more funny. The workers stood watching, throwing down orange peels.

But during the siesta, or at night, they talked of him sometimes. What would have happened, the men said softly, if we had not hit the stranger with the hammer. Would El Hombre have washed up on the beach, like a swollen seal or sea gull. Why did we hit the Mexican, to save only a tourist, for by now all the men felt the hammer in their hands. One man more or less, what did it matter, unless of course he was one's friend. "He was the butterfly's friend," said Hernando, who had a pink hibiscus in a hole in his sombrero.

So a kind of legend grew, of the man who saved damp butterflies. It grew like the afterglow of sunset. The stranger grew uglier and fiercer. The butterfly grew brighter. Part of the story they did not tell until much later. No one who had not been there was much interested. The legend did not travel far. But for the time of the Camino del Sol's building it grew. And for a little longer it persisted.

Mary Manfield's Garden

On a bright morning in late spring Mary Manfield drove her old car at a sensible pace toward the Torrey Pines Park. In most things she practiced moderation—the golden mean of not getting in the way of progress nor of outstripping it. When a ground squirrel darted in front of her she slowed and swerved, and left it room on the highway. But the roadster that passed on her left smashed the creature and roared on. Neither of the boys looked back.

"Sons of bitches," she muttered. "Sons of Caligula and Tiberius." When she turned onto the steep side road she went around the curves slowly, to allow her flow of adrenalin to subside. She knew she shouldn't get angry. At sixty-five one should have learned to accept things. No, not to accept. Nor to ignore. What was the middle way—to acknowledge?

Near the summit she parked by a pink sedan with a crumpled fender and a broken rear window. She put her entry permit card against her windshield and noticed that there was none in the other car. Then she went toward the nature trail, a path marked with identifications of the flora. She knew them all, but it always gratified her to see that something was being taught.

And as always, the smell of sun-warmed vegetation roused and soothed her, black sage and lemonade berry and buckwheat. But her mood of content as she walked along the gentle slope was jarred when she saw yellow flowers dropped on the trail—poppies and monkey flowers freshly scattered. Rounding a curve, she saw two children sliding down the soft sandstone cliff, trespassers on the forbidden rock. The sign below them read Stay on Trail. But these two were a girl about five, a boy of perhaps seven. Wildly they slid down the eroded rock face, scraping off a dust as they descended.

She stopped and smiled at them. "You must stay on the path. You mustn't go onto the rocks."

They stared at her. "Why not?" asked the boy. They were dressed in old levis and sneakers, like most California children, but their hair had not been washed lately. Nor their faces. She thought of saying sternly, "It's against the law." But the old habit of persuasion stayed with her. "The land has been injured by too many people walking on it. Now we must keep off till it has a chance to get well. And we mustn't pick the flowers, or they'll all be killed, and there won't be any more. Wouldn't that be too bad?"

"I didn't pick them, she did," said the boy.

"I did not," said the girl. "He told me to."

"Shut up," he said.

"Well, now you know not to. And you know you must stay on the path."

The smell of cigarette came over her shoulder, and she turned to face a youngish man. The beer can in his hand perhaps explained his bulging belly. The girl ran toward him. "She said we can't slide down the rocks."

"Yeah," said the boy. "She stopped us."

"What's the big idea," asked the man.

Mary pointed to the sign—Stay on Trail. "It's against the law to disturb anything in the park."

"We wasn't hurting nothing," said the boy.

She started to explain again, "The land has been damaged—"

But he cut in, taking his cigarette from his mouth and pointing it at her. "What we do is none of your business, lady."

She felt her face grow hot. "And smoking is forbidden here, because of the extreme fire hazard. You must not have seen the signs."

"I seen enough of you," he said. "What I do is my business. You take care of your kids and I'll take care of mine." He made a gesture of his arm toward her.

"Yah!" said the boy.

"Shut up," said the man.

As Mary went past him she smelled a faint stench, of flesh, sweat, tobacco, and something more, forgotten and remembered. Her narrow back felt vulnerable as she walked away, but she would not hurry. Around the next curve she met a woman walking with a child of about two. Whatever time the woman had had to prepare for this outing had been spent in arranging an enormous superstructure of coiffure. The child's bare belly stuck out above its sagging pants. They passed without speaking. Most people said good morning or hello. Some of the young ones said, "Have a nice day," and smiled.

Down from the main trail was an outlook promontory, a belvedere from which the coast was visible for many miles. There Mary sat on the bench where for years she had watched the march and retreat of waves, thinking of little skirmishes of the army of unalterable law. She discarded the idea of reporting anything to the ranger. Before she found him the people would be gone. From her vantage point she stared at the cliff which rises a sheer two or three hundred feet above the beach to a premonitory brink. The thick pinkish base of rock is thirty million years old. Above this the white limestone streak is only twenty million. On top is a thin layer of the soil of yesterday. At a few places the cliff has been eroded by wind and water and climbing feet into irregular canyons, but on the whole the face stands adamant against the western sea. To the east, the park is a narrow wild garden of shrubs and flowers and grasses, and the Torrey pines which grow nowhere else along the coast.

In the sheltered ravines, the pines grow tall and straight in little groves. But on the headlands, on the crags, clinging to the vertical rock canyons, their shapes transcend convention. Bent with the wind, pushed downward, forced and twisted, they somehow keep their roothold and survive. One lies almost prone, its roots exposed, and bears a crop of cones a few feet from the earth. In each tree can be read the history of its circumstance. Mary Manfield had read them all, with curiosity first and then compassion.

This perusal had been recreation from teaching history to high school students who did not care about anything more remote than last week or tomorrow. It had never been easy to stuff even a knowledge of events into their restless heads. Their interest was sometimes caught by the violence of battles, or the concupiscence of court intrigue, or by a flag-waving chauvinism in which it was possible briefly to hate an enemy. She had wanted to give them something more, a sense of the world's slow progress from jungle hut and kiva to flying buttresses and cantilevers. She had told them the story of Grandfather Cro-Magnon who looked at the moon with wonder and his grandsons who walked upon it. History was more than facts and dates. She had tried to fill the classroom with a sense of the great slow spread of it. She had usually failed.

After a week of such failure she had come one Saturday morning to the park and sat by a pine that had fallen along a slope, perhaps toppled by storm from the vertical which was its nature. Ripped from the soil, the roots had searched in all directions, crept into cracks, and braced themselves between bare rocks. The result was unusual, but not grotesque.

Thereafter she had gone often to the place. It was now much changed—as she was at sixty-five. But the pines were the same, smelling as they always had. Except when the jets from the air force base blared overhead, the wind in their needles sounded much the same. In the periods of silence they whispered their old dry message, that time was eternal and that courage would survive. Mary was not sure of either of these things, but she still listened.

She had plenty of time now, after a lifetime of talk, to listen and be silent. She felt she had earned her peace, after a battle. She had grown an armour to wear in the classroom: She did not expect too much and was always ready for a skirmish with indifference. She knew the students (what a misnomer) called her Bloody Mary, less a reference to the slashing of her red pencil than to the lashing of her tongue. She would rather have been called the Just, but there were worse epithets in history: the Terrible, the Mad, the Cruel.

She went to the park on week days now, when there were fewer people. She felt at home there, had images of being curled in a burrow, of sitting fluffed in sleep on a branch, of walking on alert small hooves in the moonlight. It was regression, of course. Repudiation of the world. Romanticism. But she did not really believe these words of amused appraisal. She believed in the firmness of the earth and the fragrance of the pines. Occasionally a snake would cross the path before her, and she would remember Eden, and how he was diminished. She had seen two coyotes running together, and a fox had looked at her for several minutes, holding a ground squirrel in its mouth. Rabbits hopped and listened. Sometimes there was a faint odor of skunk. She had seen footprints of deer and opossum. Squirrels came to the picnic tables. She brought bread and cookies to scatter and favored the thrashers and wrentits, that were bullied by the noisy belligerent jays. Some things need help, she thought. The park needed help now. She was glad to pay her entrance fee. It made her feel that she was helping to mark off the paths and prop old trees.

She had a hand in setting cactus to deter wanderers and putting ice plant on the unstable dunes.

Her favorite time was early in the year, when rains were followed by an amazement of wild flowers, poppies and paint brush and mallows, wild lilac and nightshade, cactus blossoms of red and gold and purple, white phlox and sisyrinchium blue as the autumn sea. But all seasons had their charms. The trees were always there, in fog or sunshine, as they had been for more than ten thousand years.

She breathed the balm of their fallen needles and tried to recover her sense of peace. The ignorant, brutal family had jarred her out of all proportion. "I think I own this place," she thought, striving to be reasonable. But her sense of outrage continued. The law-abiding should not be at the mercy of the wicked. This was the scene of the first garden, paradise invaded. This was what the situation at the park was all about, really. The innocent land, the trusting generous land, and the ancient trees, were being assaulted, ruined by dirty careless ruffians who knew nothing but to reproduce their stupid kind. The land was being raped by them.

And up from the smell of the sea spray below, and the smell of vegetation in the warm earth beside her, came the stench of the man as he had lifted his arm toward her. She sat frozen in the vault of memory. Immobilized, she was still able to count the years. Thirty-five years was not long. It was time enough for a man to have a son, and that son to have another. During all these years, while the waves gathered and fell and broke, and the sea cliffs eroded under rain and wind, another generation had had time to come to maturity and procreate its brutal young. And there would be no end of it, only an idiot repetition of meanness and violence going on forever.

I should have stopped him all those years ago, she thought. I should have had him killed, or castrated, or locked up forever. She clenched her fists, and then relaxed them, remembering how powerless they had been. She saw them now brown and ribbed like old leaves almost ready to crumble.

She had been patient with the surly boy, with his refusal to learn, his belligerent hostility, his bullying of the other students. She had reprimanded him only in private, and tried to rouse some sense of decency. He had sat slumped, fetid with flesh and tobacco. The day she saw him deliberately trip a girl and send her sprawling in the aisle, she

41

unleashed a pack of condemnation that frightened the grin from his face and sent him from the room. The principal dealt with him, and he did not return to her class.

On Friday she stayed late in a workroom, finishing a massive chart on which she hoped to show man's development of language. Carefully she copied pictographs and hieroglyphs. At thirty she was full of a desire to enrich her students, to enlarge them, to drag them upward. When she finished her chart, she stood it against the wall and turned to leave the room. Through the half-opened door a hand appeared and snapped off the light. In an instant she was thrown to the floor. Something was jammed into her mouth. Her fists were useless, her legs were pinned to the cement. She heard her clothes rip under her constricted writhing. Her teeth chewed on the rag. The force of the man's entry into her tore her flesh, but the action of his violence was brief. For an instant he was quiet. Then he lifted her head and banged it against the floor. She heard his footsteps running. The black room was full of a carnal stench.

She pulled the gag from her mouth, half choked. A bump was rising on her skull. Blood ran between her clenched legs. When she could sit up, she dragged herself to the wall and leaned back against the chart. Some of the pictographs were smeared when she swayed against it.

She remembered a dog that had been hit by a car and limped home, his eyes hopeful of care and sympathy. But where could she go? She lived alone in her new-found independence. To the police? The hospital? They would ask questions, would probe her wound. She could not endure a blazing clinical light after the horror in the darkness.

By the time her mind was clear enough for analysis, by next morning, it was too late anyway. Outraged virtue would have run screaming from the scene of the crime. It would have shouted the name of the attacker. And what followed would have been a further horror.

Can you identify the man? Yes.

Did you see him? No.

Then how can you tell? By the smell. He had a very peculiar smell.

Silence. Snickers. Odor, the most elusive of all the realities, the most evocative. But it has no vocabulary.

And what if she had been courageous, and if her charge had been proven. Public knowledge that the great hulking lout had forced her to the floor would have clothed her in ignominy, in suspicion, in pity, even in derision. She could never again have stood before her students.

Whispers would have followed her. Ghosts of rumor would have clouded all possibility that the clarity of truth could prevail in her classroom. She could not even confide in a friend, and be looked at strangely.

So she had scrubbed the blood from her limbs and been silent. On Monday she taught her classes, using the smeared chart to show man's progress from grunts and growls to the Magna Charta. Her bruised flesh healed, and her own blood had douched her clean of consequences. At times she forgot, but she remembered again, the whole affair, sitting on the sunny promontory.

When she returned to the main path, the two children were there. They had handfuls of crimson nightshade berries. The boy hid his behind him, but the girl said, "We can do what we want. We don't got to listen to you."

"Yah," said the boy, and stuck out his tongue.

"Are you going to eat the berries?" Mary asked.

"They ain't yours," the boy said, and put one in his mouth.

She walked on. To the illiterate belong the spoils. Deadly nightshade. Probably not deadly enough though. Probably only a stomachache. "Take care of your kids and I'll take care of mine." The taunt had been intended. Obviously she had none. All her children had been other people's. Deflowered by hate, she had had no progeny. No son or daughter would put flowers on her grave. No, that was rhetoric. Empty too. The worst sort. She had always planned to have her ashes spread over the sea.

When she came to the point where the trail turned inland again, she looked back toward the west, as she always did. The children were grabbing at each other's berries. Under them was the ancient rock, the newer sandstone, the recent fertile topsoil. They would never grasp the meaning of it. They would never know or care. Children of vandals, the offspring of pillagers, burners of villages, desecraters of shrines—history was full of them. They ranged from before the Sabines to the women of Bangladesh.

She stood immobile, watching the small scenario unfold before her.

The children were fighting now, picking up pebbles and dirt and throwing at each other. The girl ran and jumped over the rope that marked the path's enclosure from the cliff. The boy lunged after and followed to the edge, trampling the low white phlox. There they grappled. And then the soft earth gave way. For an instant they hung in the air before they vanished. The small white flowers wavered and were still.

Mary's throat gave a spasm of horror, but no sound came. Gagged by the enormity of it, the triviality of it, she was silent. Her mind followed the descent. How long would it take to fall three hundred feet. Her body jolted slightly and she turned away.

Apprehension touched her like a hand on her shoulder.

Did you see the children falling? Yes.

Did you try to stop them? No.

Why not? They were doomed already.

Or worse: She done it. She killed my kids. She's an old maid and hates kids. She pushed 'em off.

She would have no part in the search, would answer no questions and give no depositions. This small event in history was no concern of hers. Two more such deaths were no more important than the fall of two grains of sand. She felt as cold as God after the eviction from the garden.

But she had to stop to catch her breath after a steep place. She was not God. She was human. She was fallible and mortal. She was part of all this, rock and blue-eyed grass and pine trees, or would be for a few more earth turns. After that—She thought of her plan to have her ashes scattered on the sea. The act seemed pretentious and grandiloquent. It said nothing. Perhaps they could be buried here, dug in around the roots of the pines, mingled with the dung of coyotes, and bird droppings, and fallen needles.

But for now she would leave, before the Coiffure and the Belly started calling, ignorant of the greatness of their loss.

Mrs. Homo Sapiens

I have sat by many waters in my time. This is partly because I married a man who liked to fish. Jay doesn't fish any longer, but he still angles for money. Big money. He is insatiable. And he has netted a lot.

So I sit here on the edge of this oldest sea on a winter afternoon, looking at waters that are ruffled with wind. No yachts are out today. The tourists on the Promenade des Anglais hold their coats around them, or sit in the shelter of the bars, like me.

I am wrapped in fur and have no worries. Perhaps at my age comfort is all. The waiter brings a footstool for my feet at dinner. The maid brings a hot water bag for my bed. I am out of the wind here, looking at the Mediterranean where so much has happened. I sit thinking of what has happened to me. All I want is a waiter with wits enough to bring enough water for my tea. Aqua vitae one can get in any amount, but hot water is doled out like a prescription.

No, that is not true. I would like someone to talk to. Jay and I have said it all. My son and his wife are concerned with their own affairs. Quite rightly. My pretty, demanding grandchildren are at the age when they must learn to behave properly. I am at the age when I can do as I choose. This makes a difference between us.

And I could not tell them all the ways I have been touched by water. All they want now is to splash in it. They know nothing of depths and shallows. They have no memories. When I was about their age I stood by a flooded street, the muddy rain waters swirling up to the curbing. A policeman picked me up and carried me across. When he put me down he smiled at me. And one afternoon when I was floating paper boats at the edge of a lake in a park near my home, a man with rough grey hair came up and put his hand on my shoulder. "Come," he said, "I'll show

45

you something nice," and he crooked his finger at me, and grinned. I jerked away, and stumbled, and ran home. I never went to the park alone again.

I could list other waters, but it would be an idle game of categories, including tears and ice.

People say one loses one's memory as one ages. This isn't true. My joints have stiffened but my memory remains. I can recall the taste of bitter beer on a hot beach, and the smell of flesh, and the feel of salt on my mouth. I remember gentians blue as sapphires and columbines delicate as Mozart. The fragrance of chill wine. The lilt of birdsong. And mountain air so light and pure my body floated in it. It would be sad for these hardening bones not to have known lightness, not to have been crushed by weight. They would have nothing now but the comfort of dead fur.

They didn't need it once. They moved as freely as these palm fronds in the wind.

The woman across from me has a face like a pancake and her eyelashes aren't her own. The other day we made conversation in the lobby. She can say nothing in three languages. If I mentioned the waters of life she would tell me about the spa where she goes for her liver. "Wonderful—horribly expensive but worth every franc—The Duchess de non Gout is devoted to it!"

There are people who understand symbols and those who don't. Again I play my game of categories. I don't think Jay has ever realized why he wanted to catch all those fish. If he had not wanted them, if he had been content with his job, and the country club, and me—he would have missed a lot. But God knows what it is he had from it all, besides exercise and something to talk about. He could tell you the weight and length of everything he ever hooked.

He was always very attractive, in an average, middle-sized, agreeable way. People used to say we were a handsome pair. It used to make me feel like a couple of vases. But vases don't couple. Jay never liked me in my bawdy moments. Body moments? He was never interested in word play. Playing a bass on the end of a line was what enthralled him. I should have been a mermaid. A meremaid. I was mere woman.

A few years after we married we spent his vacation in the mountains. We had a one-room cabin, very crude, among pine trees, no plumbing or hot water, and I cooked on a wood fire. It was pleasant in spite of being so primitive. Jay fished for trout all day and I read and walked around.

One morning after he left with his rod and lunch I looked at the rumpled bunks and the egg yolk hardening on the plates, and the hovel felt like a place for troglodytes to breed in. Jay left it everyday for his ponds and riffles. I felt I must leave it too. I tidied the surface and myself and closed the door. As soon as I was outside I expanded with the morning, like a chick that rolls out of its broken shell.

I followed a trail to the lake and crossed a meadow. The ground was moist, and blue flowers were growing close to it, cups like enormous sapphires. I sat on a log to look at them, and then up to a mountain of unmoving pines, and further to the bright blue sky. The fragrance of morning swept through me and I felt glad—more than that, exultant—at being alive and in that place. Such ecstasy comes sometimes out of nothing. I have felt it often. But not lately.

I had been musing there for I don't know how long when a man we had met at the Ranger's house came by. He was tall and lean, and his curly blond hair was ringed with sunshine. "What are you looking at?" he asked.

"The flowers. What are they?"

"Gentians. They like these damp spots." He sat on the log beside me, a man about fifty with clear blue eyes. It was very companionable. We just sat there sharing the morning. When a bird sang a sudden trilling melody we looked at each other. "A white-crowned sparrow," he said.

"Do you know everything?"

"No. But I try to know as much as I can."

We sat awhile longer. "Look," he said, and pointed upward. "A golden eagle." The bird was not high. I could see the sun gleam on its wings as it sailed, slowly circling. Then it rose, lifting and lifting until its shape was lost.

"It takes me with it a little," I said, feeling a little embarrassed for myself.

"It should. The eagle has always been a symbol of man's aspiration. He lifts us with his wings." It was then that he invited me to have lunch with him in his house across the lake. I accepted without question.

We crossed the water in a canoe. I remember the sense of ease as he paddled, and the lightness and balance of the craft as we glided past yellow water lilies. I sat very still until we landed, and then he smiled and helped me jump out.

His house was a surprise. From outside it was an ordinary mountain cabin, but entering was like stepping within the walls of an old stone church and finding new washed lace and fresh flowers on the altar. We listened to a Mozart record while I helped prepare our lunch. At a table overlooking the lake we had cold pheasant and strawberries and a bottle of white wine. There were white columbines in a celadon bowl, nature shaped in a mood as sophisticated as the music. "How very civilized this is," I said.

"Man does not live by bread alone, but the bread he eats should be the best."

As we lingered at the table he told me about the dark wooden statue on a shelf, a female with hanging breasts and a bulging belly. A fertility image. And then I looked again at the picture of the Madonna holding her Child on the opposite wall. The Infant clutched a bright yellow bird with a crimson head. "A goldfinch," he said. "The bird was the symbol of the soul for the religious painters. As it still is." For he saw that I was ignorant. Ignorant and young. Quietly he explained how man has lived by symbols because they compress abundance into a usable shape, something that can be grasped through repeated experience of meaning. When we see the baby holding the bird we know it is not merely a child with a goldfinch. If we are oriented to the symbol, we feel a lift of salvation. The bird's wings lift us. As the eagle's did. And when we look at the breasts and belly and deep cleft of the dark African female, we know something of dark fecund nature, out of which we came. A symbol is an essence. That is really all.

"As wine is compressed from grapes?" I asked, tasting something more than grapes in my glass.

He accepted my inadequate analogy. "Yes. Because symbols are not rigid. And wine has many uses—for everything from bacchanals to sacraments. And for toasts to happy chance meetings."

He paid me no compliment beyond the raising of his glass. But I felt more beautiful when I left him. By accepting me into his house he made me part of the symmetry of Mozart and the intricacy of columbines. I have been flattered, before and since. But that day the world and I were enlarged.

When I grew large with pregnancy a few years later, the sheer physical fact was enough to content me. In a glaring white room the amniotic waters burst and I bore my son. We both cried, he with fury after his travail, I with joy after mine. Then I nursed and fondled him like any other

48

mammal. And later lost him to himself.

I never lost Jay completely. And never really had him. Oh, we have been as close as most. Mr. and Mrs. James Wolf—residents of reputable neighborhoods, respecters of conventions, supporters of good causes, subscribers to the Wall Street Journal and Harper's Bazaar—we have walked and dined and slept together, without great discord or notoriety. It wasn't always easy. We were brought together by the heat of youth and then were fused in matrimony. Fused and confused. Or I was. Refused too. How neatly the sly mind makes its connections. Some of the things I was refused I didn't even realize at the time.

One winter Jay and I went to Mexico with two other couples. The men wanted to go after swordfish. Every day for a week they went out in a boat. They caught several monsters and had their pictures taken, and strutted like conquistadores. We women swam and lay around in hammocks. In the evening we drank tequila or rum. The men were gallant and a little romantic. We females were flirtatious and coy and laughed a lot under the palm huts on the beach.

After a few days I got so rested that I started staying awake at night. Jay slept after all his exercise. I listened to the wind in the palm leaves and the waves pounding the shore. Somewhere a burro yearned for something. A cat prowled and called, urgent and feral. One morning I got up very early and walked inland among coconut trees on a dusty road. A huge green iguana ran in front of me and climbed a trunk. I looked and saw others, almost hidden in the roughness of the fronds. They were grey or green, with irregular spines and crests, and tiny alert eyes. I thought they looked back at me out of their strangeness. And I remembered that their family was older than mine.

When I got back to the hotel, the rest were eating breakfast. "I took a walk," I explained. "I saw iguanas."

"The Mexicans eat them," said one of the men.

"Ugh," said one of the women. "How awful. I couldn't."

"No," I said, "it would be like eating a relative." They didn't know what I meant. I hardly did myself.

"Are you hung over?" Jay asked. "Give her some coffee."

All day peddlers walked along the beach in front of the hotel and tourists idly haggled over their baskets or weaving. Every day a boatman offered a trip along the coast or to the islands a few miles off shore. "No, gracias," we said, and watched him go and return with others. But I thought about it. I wondered what was out there—if anything. From the crowd and clutter of the hotel's private beach, the far cliffs looked remote and alluring.

The day before we left Mexico, the other women went shopping. I went to the beach as usual. When the boatman came, I asked how far the island directly westward was. A mile or so. Could we go to the other side? Of course. We agreed on a price, and he would take a lunch for us. We met on the shore an hour later.

I watched him launch the little boat. He was not a tall man, but broad. His dark skin was smooth, as if polished by the sea. We were both beyond youth, but he looked ageless as he pushed us from the shore and swung aboard. The tide was coming in and the boat leaped and dropped over the small waves, the motor throbbing noisily. Then it settled to a purr. I watched the diminishing coast and then looked westward. The island was shaped like a huge saurian, half submerged and sleeping. The small head was lowered, the back rose sharply, covered with irregular spines, and sloped its length into the water. As we approached, it seemed to rouse with the motion of the waves. The illusion vanished as we got closer, and I could see the stalks of agave along the summit.

When we reached the far side of the island we came upon dolphins, two of them swimming slowly, their sharp curved fins rising above the water, and then the arc of their backs, up and down in a rhythm like deep breathing. They came near and we stopped to watch them. It seemed to me that they looked at us. "They are good omens," he said.

"How wonderful to have them so close."

"Si. They are not afraid of us." For awhile longer they dipped and circled. "They are the friend of man. All my life I have heard stories of how they have helped seamen in trouble by leading them to shore. I have not seen it, but I have heard." They left us, curving up and down as if their strength had no end.

We landed on a sandy beach. While he took things from the boat I walked along the shore and climbed over rocks to a promontory. The hot sun of noonday glazed the empty horizon. The whole surface of the sea was burnished free of life. The effect was of an immense isolation. Or timelessness. Or both.

He had spread a brown serape under a tree in deep shade by the cliff. He smiled and handed me a bottle of beer. "You like it here?"

"It is very nice. One can forget the world."

"The world does not come here. It is too wild still."

He had brought ham sandwiches from the hotel. We drank more beer and he peeled oranges for me. Lulled and fed, I closed my eyes. "I'm sleepy," I said. "I can't stay awake."

"Si. It is time for the siesta." And we both lay back on the blanket. I dropped at once into blackness and could feel myself falling in a dizzy descent before I was lost.

When I woke, he was sitting up looking at me. It was as if he had always been there, waiting, and at last I had found him. His mouth was soft and speechless. He made no avowals. I made no protestations. I was pressed between the hardness of earth and the hardness of his body, in an embrace as candid as sunshine. Our passion grew and I could not have denied it, whatever the consequences. If this was the end of me and the end of the world, so be it. And I surged farther away from myself and into myself then I had ever been.

Afterward we were still silent and walked on the beach hand in hand, our feet in the shore splash. By a submerged boulder the water deepened and we stood up to our knees in it. "Look," he said, and I saw fishes, tiny silver slivers like glints of moonlight. Each was marked with a line of dark along its length, each was as perfectly made as if it were unique. But there were thousands darting and swirling. The world seemed infinitely abundant, full of such richness. Whatever made them was tireless and bountiful. It would survive. We watched until some impulse made them vanish.

When the sun made a path on the water I said, "I must go back."

"To the world."

"Yes." The word hissed in my mouth as if my flesh was outraged. When we rounded the island and I saw the far shore I felt I could not face it. But there was no choice. I could not swim out to sea, following the dolphins. The waters of our return were quiet, and I grew resigned. He helped me from the boat. When I reached in my bag to pay him, and hesitated, he helped me again.

"Only the price as agreed, Senora."

"Gracias."

"Gracias." We both smiled and turned away.

The men had had bad luck. Jay had lost a big one. The women had spent all day in shops and were loaded with stuff. They jabbered all through dinner. Next day we left for home.

I never knew the name of the island. I never knew his name. His boat was El Delfin. Even now I am glad that for once in all my careful days I was a thing of impulse, mindless as a seed pod in the wind. Or a dolphin mating.

At different times in life one wants such different things. Once my greatest desire was for pretty dresses, to costume myself for what I thought I was. I have been a princess and a peasant in my day. Not for long, but long enough to know how it felt. And it had nothing to do with the way I looked. When I was a princess I was wearing slacks and my hair was tied back with an old ribbon. When I was a peasant I slipped out of a dress with a famous label, so expensive that it could afford to look like nothing.

One needs such different things. Comfort is not enough. One still needs human contact. The waters of life may run slow, but they have not dried up. I would like someone to talk to. A woman who isn't a fool. A girl I knew in college maybe, or earlier, when we were growing up, and silly, and fearful. We might even still giggle, in between telling the truth for once. We didn't know what it was then, when we sat drying our hair in the sunshine. Now we go to the beauty parlor and come out fashionable and frizzled. Some of us talk to the hair dresser, but that is only nervous chatter. What I want is someone to say something to.

But what? That I have been married and had a child? That I have been miserable and happy? That our dreams possess us, but we possess our daydreams to the end?

I could not speak of my journeys over water. They are trips to the center of my inmost world where need is naked and honest as a baby's cry. My querulous words would cancel them. So I talk to myself—Mrs. Homo sapiens. Wife of Mr. Know-it-all, who walks the earth as if it was a golf course. Temporary inhabitant of terra firma. Mrs. Homo infirma. But not completely. Not yet. By this sea where so much has happened, nothing happens to me now. I sit drinking hot water flavored with dry leaves.

The Loiterer

Irving Bott had never wanted to be part of the action. Even as a boy he had been content to sit in the stands, watching. When he was late coming home from school his mother would say, "What have you been doing?" He was a fattish child, and she thought he needed to move around more.

He would reply, "Nothing."

"What do you mean, nothing?"

"Just looking around."

But he was a good boy and the only time he came anywhere near getting in trouble was when a woman phoned the police to say a kid was looking in her bedroom window. It was broad daylight and Irv was still sitting on a low wall watching some ants struggle over a caterpillar when the patrol men arrived. They warned him, and put a few ideas in his head. But he didn't use them.

Much later he had a brief difficulty with the law when his wife Cora died. While they were driving home from a vacation, she suddenly collapsed. No highway car came to his aid, and he drove on with Cora beside him. He might have made it to a hospital but had to stop for a state agricultural inspection.

For a while thereafter he missed the bars of domesticity. He was like a middle-sized bear that had been loosed from his cage and did not know where to go. He looked a little like a bear, a fattish man of medium height, rather slow to get started and content to sit contemplating the world. Cora had often complained that he never wanted to do anything. So one anniversary they took a trip to Las Vegas. They went to some shows. Cora lost fifty-four dollars gambling. Irving just walked around the casinos looking. He had a good time too. The eyes of the gamblers were very hot. The eyes of the dealers were very cold.

Cora had always been crazy about the movies. When they first met and after they were married, Irving took her once or twice a week. He had been crazy about Cora. As time and the celluloid unrolled he found it less thrilling to sit holding hands, watching enormous people for whom he had no empathy or sympathy. One day he refused to go. Cora looked cute and provocative in the Hollywood style of 1940. "That's the way men are, no interest in the finer things of life," she pouted. It did no good.

From then on Cora usually attended matinees. At dinner she recounted the plot to Irving. After a while this bored the hell out of him. But it was rather interesting to watch Cora, whose coiffure and expression and voice changed with the fashions of the leading ladies. Even when television came along she missed the wider screen. Irving sometimes took her and a friend downtown to one of the big theatres. He wandered around until time to bring them home. One night his feet hurt him. He stayed in the car, watching the people. That was when his real life started. He was fifty.

After that he looked forward to sitting in the car watching the passersby as much as Cora did entering the Paramount or the Uptown. It turned out that they were both entranced by patterns. Cora loved to love the heroine and hate the villain. She thrilled to violence and happy endings. Irving's sidewalk scenes had none of this finality. He saw things in flashes and fragments. Even so, patterns emerged. Usually the people were pretty ordinary. But they suggested something—an immemorial sameness, humanity at its peak of mediocrity. That was part of the truth revealed to him, that for most of the world nothing much ever happened.

He saw it memorably in a woman who leaned on the window sill of a second floor apartment one evening. She had big breasts under a pink buttoned sweater and rested them on her folded arms. For a long time she sat there, only her eyes moving, up and down the street, perusing something. Sometimes the woman's glance met his own but neither acknowledged the encounter.

There were other confirmations. The old men who walked around the block at evening, in felt slippers or shoes split at the sides, shuffling and nodding their heads, all looked alike in a grey and wrinkled way. They talked to themselves. Sometimes there was a tenth of whiskey in the sagging jacket pocket. They vanished into doorways with signs like

Hope Hotel, Monthly Rates. Cora would have called them skid row bums. Irving had no name for them.

He did have a name for the women he called Maggies, after a friend of his mother. He noticed that old ladies, a special sort, spend a long time preparing their faces when they go out. They put on layers of makeup, filling in the wrinkles, carefully drawing dark curved eyebrows, circling rouge on their saggy cheeks. They balance their hats neatly and walk with head erect, a little red smile on their thin lips. But below the neck they have lost interest. Their stockings wrinkle, their shoes are run over, and their petticoats hang down in back. Every time he saw one, he'd chuckle. There's another. But when he told Joe and Liz Harper about them once, nobody understood. Joe said, "Aren't you a little old to be looking at ladies' petticoats, Irv?" Liz and Cora glanced at each other.

Cora quickly said it was pathetic the way some old women tried to hang on to their youth, using rouge and all. Afterward she asked, "What was all that about the old women?" He tried to explain how it was just interesting the way people fell into types that kept recurring, so you could recognize them. It made you feel there was a point to things, somehow, to spot a familiar one, like a Maggie. This was either too simple or too complex for Cora.

After her unconventional demise, he arranged for an expensive funeral. It seemed only right that she should star in a good production. After a time he adjusted to his solitary state and at sixty settled into a quiet content.

He parked one evening on a street with two movie theatres. In one direction was the Gem. On the marquee were advertised The Dog Faced Rapist & Knee Deep in Blood—You'll Scream With Horror. Around the sign was a dizzying row of moving lights. Almost in front of him the Rialto advertised Double Feature—Dregs of Love & A Virgin in Sodom. A large photograph of an almost nude female in a strange pose looked at the queue of ticket buyers from between her knees. A three-year-old holding his mother by the hand stared back at her.

After a while Irving thought he had a pretty good idea of what is meant by a motley crowd. Out of it a young woman in magenta shorts came up to his window. She smiled. "Do you want to buy—anything?"

"No thanks," said Irving.

"I've got—anything you want. Anything at all."

"No thanks." The woman stood there a moment and then returned to the sidewalk. Irving thought of a slogan popular in his youth, Life in the raw is seldom mild. It seemed to him that the woman in magenta pants looked pretty mild compared to the actress pictured outside the box office.

He watched the woman while she approached a man who was lounging along as if he had all night to spare. After a few words the man grabbed her wrist and flipped open his coat. She struggled and said, "Lemme go." A police car slid out of an alley and the woman was thrust inside. "Lemme go," she screamed. "You got nothing on me." But the door slammed behind her. "Luck," thought Irving. If he had accepted her proposal, she wouldn't be riding in a patrol car now. Or maybe they both would. He shook his head. He wondered if whores were mostly actresses who couldn't make it. They had to have some talent, act interested, keep trouping, learn their lines. How much depends on luck: you end up on a stage being applauded, or in bed in a back room with somebody like—Irving Bott. It was frightening in a way.

Starting to back his car from the stall, he looked into the rear view mirror and saw a helmeted head and two eyes staring at him. Then the head vanished and a motorcycle roared away.

A few nights later, Irving parked his car on State Street, leaned back comfortably, and looked through the windshield. The dusty smell of the pavement, the exhaust fumes of buses, the odor of humanity, seemed as appropriate as the smells of old velour and tobacco and popcorn in a third-rate theatre. People walked before him from right or left. Even the motions of their passage varied, as if each was hinged or strung up differently. The business man had an extra tenseness in his elbow. The fat woman was slightly disjointed in the pelvis. Mostly the characters were the usual ones. The hippies were as standardized as the soldiers, but three men in saffron robes and shaved heads were exotics. A small tableau shaped up, a man pushing a woman in a wheelchair, her legs in braces. They stopped at her word to look into a window of dresses. As she stared—dreaming bitterly of wearing pink satin, blue chiffon?—the man glanced covertly at two girls in shorts. When the woman spoke to him he started and jerked his head. What hours of guilt and yearning would follow, had preceded, this small scene, Irving wondered. What violence might grow out of it. His eyes became unfocused in the mist of speculation.

"OK, Mac, what a ya think you're doing?" The loud words jolted

Irving and he looked at the policeman who was staring at him through the open car window.

"Nothing," said Irving, but he felt his flesh creep, cold in the summer air. "I'm just sitting here. Minding my own business."

"I've had my eye on you." Irving could believe it. The policeman's eye was hardly a foot from his own. He looked slightly cross-eyed. But the effect was not comic. Irving pulled himself up out of his comfortable slouch. The flag on the parking meter said Violation, but it was after six o'clock. "I've had my eye on you for several weeks now."

"What for?"

"That's what I want to know. What are you sitting here for?"

"I'm just looking."

"What are you looking at?"

"People."

"What kind of people?"

"Just—people. The ones that go by. Anybody."

"What for?"

"Well—I just like to watch them, that's all."

"What do you like to watch them for?"

Irving took a deep breath. "I am interested in the human race. Its activities. Its appearance. Its habits." The policeman seemed not to hear. He went on down his list.

"You look at women?"

"Sure. Some of the time."

"What kind of women?"

"All kinds. Big ones, little ones, young ones, old ones. I look at men too!"

"What kind of men are you looking for?"

"I'm not looking for any kind. I'm just looking at any kind that comes along. Big ones, little ones, young ones, old ones."

"Wise guy, huh. What do you look at them *for*?"

"I told you. I like to think about them." Irving leaned toward the policeman. "They're like people in a play. They do things. Only not exactly like in a play. Nothing really happens to them. They just go along, being themselves." He tried to smile at the face in the window.

"Then why don't you go to the movies, where something does happen? Or watch TV?"

"I don't like movies."

"What's wrong with movies?"

"They bore the hell out of me."

"You married?"

"My wife is dead." Irving said it coldly. He had an impulse to add, "Maybe you think I killed her?" But he didn't. His statement seemed to make the policeman a little less hostile.

"Look, Mac, I'm trying to help you. I don't want to run you in. You aren't exactly a vagrant. You aren't exactly loitering. But you are acting very very funny."

"I don't see anything funny about me. I'm minding my own business."

"You can't tell what is anybody's business. We got a drive on to anticipate crime and prevent it. Don't you read the papers either?"

"What kind of a crime is sitting in my car?"

"I don't know—yet. Guys like you could be a pusher. Or a pimp. Or a voy-yoor."

"A what?"

"A voy-yoor. A Peeping Tom. Only you don't look in bathroom windows, you look out a car window. You just—might—be a voy-yoor."

"Now wait a minute. I resent that Peeping Tom business. I'm no pervert!"

"I'm not saying you are, I'm not saying you aren't. I'm just warning you."

"Since when—"

"And you're taking up space from legitimate car drivers."

"A parking place is a parking place. I don't see it matters if I sit in my car or don't sit in it."

"Look Mac, I'm warning you. Two or three times a week you sit and stare at people. It's not healthy. You ought to see a psychiatrist and get straightened out. And I'm going to keep my eye on you." He vanished, and Irving heard the sputter of a motorcycle engine.

When he entered his own back door, he stood for a moment looking around the clean neat kitchen. The humming of the refrigerator was suddenly loud at his back. He turned as if accosted and sighed. Me. A pervert. He took a bottle of beer, uncapped it violently, and went into the living room. As he drank, his anger drained from him, but he felt frightened and chagrined. He was a small fat boy who had been unjustly reprimanded. And what if he was a loiterer? What was so wrong about that? Why shouldn't he loiter in his own home town? Since when was looking at people a crime, or even a misdemeanor?

Damn O'Clanahan, thought Irving, emptying his bottle. I suppose he would understand it if I was a drunk. He's used to drunks. He imagined himself spending his evenings at a tavern watching the other drunks. A lonely drinker would attract another lonely drinker. The second drinker would want to talk. Irving wouldn't want to talk. There would be drunken words. Irving would have to leave. Even if all the drinkers were quietly watching television, a boxing match or football, there wouldn't be much of interest. Irving looked at Cora's TV set. He turned it on. A man in tight pants, an enormous hat and two guns, was leering at a girl more outside of than inside of a frilly white blouse. He turned the dial. Two men were lunging and kicking each other, emitting grunts and roars. He tried again. A man woke in his bed and saw the bloody head of a horse beside him. He clicked the scene to a pinpoint of nothingness.

He sat on his bed with one shoe off, considering. Why were canned entertainments so boring. Even if you liked blood, the way some people like catsup over everything. They were like TV dinners. Somebody measured them out, and smeared them on plastic, and advertised them as the real thing. They weren't the real thing. The people in them had only one side, the side facing the audience. The other side, the unknown, unpredictable, real side of people, you never saw. That, by God, was it. The writer stacked everything to show the side he wanted. The audience couldn't get behind all that to get their own view.

Lying in bed he thought further. People on the street weren't finished. Something in them was not yet ended. They were still happening. And he could watch it. Tomorrow, he vowed, lifting his hand heavenward and sticking his chin up, he'd find that minion of the law and spell it out. But he knew he wouldn't. O'Sullivan was just a television cop. He saw himself as a stern defender of society, whatever that was. Whatever it was, it did not include Irving.

He visualized himself parked on State Street. How would he appear to someone else, an onlooker. He was a man of sixty, decently dressed, well fed and underexercised, with no noticeable marks of difference or achievement on him. What was he waiting for—a love of his youth, a girl he had lost through mischance or someone else's skill in love? Or was he waiting, lurking, for some private enemy to appear? Or for someone he himself had wronged, on an asphalt playground, or a highway, or a battle field, from whom he must ask forgiveness? Was he merely a husband, waiting for his wife to make a decision, or match a piece of fabric of an unmatchable blue. Or was the tank out of gas, the rear tire flat, the battery dead, and the foot on the accelerator paralyzed.

Next morning as he ate his fried eggs Irving went over his situation. He could park somewhere else. But Casey, or O'Riley, or whoever he was, would pass the word along to watch out for him. A crackpot. An incipient criminal. A voyeur, for God's sake. He considered other alternatives. He could move away, to another town. But after awhile he would again be pursued. He would move again. He saw himself being pushed off the map. When he backed his car out of the garage to go to work, the man across the street waved. A block later he wondered if he was being spied on. That night when a siren suddenly accused the silence around his house, he held his breath. He could almost remember a quotation that had been popular for a while. Something like Ask not for whom the Black Maria comes, it comes for thee.

For some time Irving worked on his problem. He went to the Savoy Lobby and watched the comings and goings. Men on business trips. With their wives on conventions. Or their secretaries. Women traveling on their husbands' insurance. People with imported overcoats and briefcases and ulcers, and diamonds and resort folders and wrinkles. He had to dress up, not to be conspicuous against the plush and pillars. He went to the railroad station, where people were hurrying and saying good-bye. He sat in the park among the derelicts and pigeons. When he smiled at a little girl, her mother rushed and snatched the child away with an ugly look at him. In restaurants, he had to eat. In stores, people tried to sell him something. In church, everyone wore the same washed Sunday face. None of these frequented places would do. He needed a reserved seat, where he could see through the windshield of his vision the eternal parade, unpicked, uncontrived, flowing without script or plot across his stage.

He would have liked to talk about the incident with the cop to somebody. But he could see the men at the office tapping their foreheads. The Harpers would remember the old ladies. He had a cousin who had a farm and liked to lean on the fence staring at his cows, meditating, chewing on a piece of grass, just vaguely looking at the growing fields and calves. But that wasn't the same. The cousin would say, "Come on out and live in the country. I told you it's not healthy living on concrete.

It'll get you."

One evening he read an article about moonlighting. Things were very bad. Even the police were taking two jobs to make ends meet. "Of course," he said. He jumped to his feet and circled the room in a bearish dance. Next day he went to see his lawyer. Afterward he walked down the street chuckling out loud. People turned to stare at him. Anyone idly waiting in a car would have wondered.

A few nights later he parked again downtown. There were clouds overhead and occasional flashes of lightning in the west. Soon a rain started and people rushed by holding newspapers over their heads, and Irving went home. He felt as if he had been to a rehearsal that was shaping up nicely.

After dinner next day he found a parking place down toward the small business district. Part of the freedom of his outings was the element chance played in them. Wherever and whenever he parked, the action started. There was no curtain time.

In front of him was Dave's New & Used Clothes. A dark bearded man stood in the doorway with his hands in his pockets. Irving reached in the glove case and took out a thick notebook, a pencil, and a small counter and put them on the seat. He wondered about the man in the doorway. Maybe he came from a European ghetto, where he had lived in fear and privation. Maybe he had been in a concentration camp. Perhaps his sweetheart had been killed. Or they had escaped together, to cross a stormy Atlantic and start life in a free country, where there was no Gestapo and every man could do as he liked. "Humph," Irving snorted. Then he looked at the little counting gadget beside him.

When it happened, he was looking at two women, obviously mother and daughter. He could see the work of twenty years in wrinkles and saggings on the older one. Do they ever look at each other and feel how cruel time is, he wondered.

"Hi, Mac." Irving looked up. It was his cue.

"Good evening," he said.

"Haven't seen you for awhile," said the policeman.

"No." Irving looked O'Clanahan in the eye.

"What are you looking for tonight?"

"Red shoes."

"What?"

"Red shoes."

"Don't try to be funny with me."

"I am not being funny. I am looking for red shoes."

"Yeah? What're you going to do with them when you get them?"

"I'm not going to do anything with them. I am merely counting them."

The cop's face got red. Then he became violently restrained. "Look, I've been very patient with you, but when you start insulting the law—"

"I'm not insulting anybody. You ask me a question, I answer you."

"I ask a sensible question, you give a crazy answer. I could run you in for loitering."

"Pardon me," said Irving, craning his head out of the window to look at a woman going by. "No, sorry, they're pink."

"What are pink?"

"Her shoes."

"Look," said the cop. Irving decided the dialogue had gone on long enough.

"Listen, I'll try to explain it. I am counting the incidence of red shoes worn this summer by females in a typical middle-sized city. This I am doing for a shoe manufacturer who wants to know if red shoes are popular. I count the shoes. I send him the information. He knows if he wants to make red shoes or not. Simple as that."

"Well, yeah, but—" He was not vanquished. "Is this all you do?"

"Not at all. I gather all kinds of information, depending on the need. I am a statistician." Irving reached in his pocket and pulled out a card. He handed it to the policeman. J. Irving Bott, Statistician, was centered on the card. Down in one corner, in smaller type, was the word Confidential.

The policeman stood holding the card. His eye roved over Irving and the car. He noted the small object on the seat. Irving glanced at it too. "That," he said, "is a counter. I just press here. The number pops up here. Saves time."

"Sure does." He handed the card back to Irving. "Look—why did you spiel that cock and bull story about watching people?"

"Special assignment. Confidential." Irving winked slowly. "What did you say your name was?"

"Zyhofski." Irving blinked. "OK, Mr. Bott. Be seeing you."

Irving heard the pop and snarl of his motorcycle, and then the diminishing howl. Sinking comfortably down in the driver's seat, he felt the house lights dimming around him.

Forsaking All Others

Watching the man and woman on the little dance floor in the restaurant, Margaret thought she had never seen anyone look happier. Not brides, or children on Christmas morning, or dogs chasing sticks. They danced with accustomed ease, his big brown arm holding her firmly, their faces close and smiling. They weren't doing any young funny stuff like even some of the oldsters, swinging around and walking away and coming back and looking complacent about the manoeuvers. They were doing old-fashioned steps, belly to belly, thigh to thigh, and laughing. They were fortyish and her figure wasn't very good. She had probably had a couple of children. But her face was pretty. Any face that happy would be pretty. And he was obviously perfectly content to be looking into it. When they came back to their table Margaret noted that the man wore a wedding ring too.

The music the Mexican played on the crude organ was loud and schmaltzy. But again and again the middle-aged pair abandoned their food to cling and swirl in it. That was what a vacation south of the border could do to married people. When they left home they locked the door on habit and went forth into newness, and felt new, and their spouses were new too. Or refurbished.

When the musician went off to drink a Coca Cola, talk was again possible. Margaret looked at her own husband, long enduring and endured. He was enjoying his carne asada. From the little charcoal broiler between them he lifted a choice piece and held it toward her. That was part of marriage, sharing the bad and giving the best. "The marriage service should be rewritten," she said. "With this hand I promise always to give you the tenderest meat."

"Until death do us part or your teeth fall out, whichever comes first," said Daniel.

"I think I'm serious," she said.

"Your nose is seriously sunburned. But I'll ask you to dance anyway when the meat is eat."

They danced chest to chest too, though impeded by a couple that was wheeling and flinging each other around while looking as if they were following an obscure pattern mandated by a rather bored and boring fate. The happy couple was leaning together across their table, talking. That was another trouble with marriage, one ran out of conversation. An advantage to having children was that one could always talk about them. And one could look around, appraising the way other women had weathered or been weathered by the years. And wondering why they had married that one. Had they simply taken whatever was tossed them, like a hungry pelican? It looked as if the woman in the lilac pants suit had something stuck in her throat.

Other couples had this problem. They brightened up when there were two pairs. A fresh audience for everybody. Even so, it was hard to look enchanted when one's spouse again told about that hilarious thing that happened on the boat, much funnier than it had really been, and quite different. Of course one could always ask questions. Once she had asked, "What was the happiest day of your life?" Instantly he had said, "The day I got my first driver's license." It had meant freedom. When he enquired, "What was yours?" mostly out of politeness she thought, she said, "I was younger. It was the day I found out about birth control." Neither mentioned the day they got their marriage license. That had been a giving up of freedom. Thereafter, from that day forward, they had forsaken total honesty.

The Mexican girl with the enormous eyes and earrings, over there, was looking at her escort. He was very serious—demanding? explaining? entreating? She tapped salt on her lime, sucked it, sipped tequila, looked again at the man. How wonderful to be young, brunette, squeezing lime on one's tongue, on the verge of accepting or refusing something.

"Do you ever want to be someone else?" Margaret asked.

"Mohammed Ali? Prince Charles? Liz Taylor's eighth husband? Let me think."

"We should write in the marriage ceremony 'I promise not to be frivolous when my spouse is serious and not to be serious when she's

66

frivolous.'"

"How can you tell?"

"You get to know if you're a proper husband."

"I'll put in 'I promise not to be bugged by non sequiturs, till confusion does us part.'"

They ate their flan slowly. There were no non sequiturs really. On the level below words, down deep, a constant flow of perceptions pushed everything along. Everything mingled and became one in this unending river that was one's life. Nothing was lost. It was simply that some things weren't noticed. Margaret was feeling too drowsy to try to explain. Certainly she wasn't going to explain why the dark girl sipping tequila and sucking limes drew her attention. The happy couple was leaving the lighted restaurant, walking into the dark of a greater closeness.

Margaret saw them walking on the path next morning, hands swinging together. Later they lay on the beach in bathing suits, not touching but somehow joined in an accustomed way of life. Daniel would say this was another of her groundless inferences if she put it in words. So she was silent and felt certain. When the pair swam out in the bay they went together like two sea lions cruising. Margaret promised herself that she would be more courageous in the sea. This time she meant it. She really did.

The happy couple was in the restaurant again that evening, drinking dark wine. After some moments of silence they suddenly lifted their glasses and drained them and went to the dancing space. They moved perhaps less gaily than the night before, more in a quiet symmetry, but smiling at each other. They were alone on the floor.

"What are you staring at?" asked Daniel.

"The couple dancing. They look so happy."

"Margaritas no doubt."

"You're a cynic. Or do I mean skeptic?"

"I'm a sybarite. I buy you enchiladas and beer."

"Before we were married you promised me pheasant and champagne."

"That was before I learned that two cannot live as cheaply as one."

"Knowledge is always expensive," she said after biting into her enchilada. "But I'll give you some for nothing. This sauce is damned hot."

He took a bite to see for himself and swallowed. Manfully, the

67

expression was. Why should she worry about his digestion, when he never took her advice. Though her worrying would seem to be part of the cherishing she had promised to do. When he could speak, Daniel said, "I was hearing about a guy from Texas who put a big slug of vodka in his wife's Margarita, thinking she'd get too fuzzy to notice he had his eye on a senorita. But the wife switched glasses and he got sloshed and when he asked the senorita to dance and stared into her cleavage she slapped him. They went home next day."

That was one nice thing about Daniel. He didn't mind it when the male turned out to be the jerk. Some men only told stories about stupid wives. "You are more precious than rubies," she said.

"Don't mention it," he said, but nothing about non sequiturs.

The happy pair was sitting over their coffee. The woman picked up a spoon and stirred hers, as if she was thinking of something else. When the man spoke to her she looked up, and smiled and nodded. Clearly it was the end of a long sun-filled day. They drank their coffee and went again into the night.

Next day dawned as blue and calm as ever, like Eden before the fall. Margaret said as much to Daniel. "You say that every morning," he said.

"It's true every morning," she replied and started cooking break-fast in the tiny kitchenette of their apartment.

He said, "I'll be back in a minute," and wandered off. When the meal was ready he had not returned. He was not visible from the balcony. Vanished. Again. Gone into some thoughtless and inconsiderate world of his own while she stirred his food and dangled, waiting. The eggs got cool and her temper got warm. When he finally came back, she didn't look at him.

"Anybody would think you could develop some sense of time," she said, hearing her voice rising like a seagull's but unable to stop it, pushed along in the wind of her annoyance. "After all these centuries mankind ought to have evolved some idea of time passing."

"I'm not all mankind. And I refuse to have my life ruled by some-body else's time sense."

The morning ritual of the breaking of bread was made in silence. I could go home, she thought. I could get on a plane and leave. But she didn't say it. What if he replied, "Go ahead." Don't present ultimatums unless you are prepared for the ultimate one.

Presently he handed her the honey jar, translating from the label—

Miel de Abeja, bee-honey. "This is very good. Have some." He didn't say, "This will sweeten your disposition."

Mollified—mielified?—she said, "Why don't you write the kids a postcard and we'll walk down and mail it."

"What'll I tell them?"

"Tell them not to talk to any strange snakes."

When they got to the motel office an ambulance was parked outside. So was a police car. People were standing around inside. Daniel asked, "What's happened?"

A fat man holding a yellowtail at the gills said, "A man died in the night. A heart attack apparently."

"Who was it?"

"A guy from Arizona. Name of Belett. There'll be a lot of red tape. His wife will have to fly down."

"Was he alone?"

"He was with his lady friend. She's talking to the police over there."

Margaret looked where the man indicated. The female half of the happy couple was sitting at a table with a man in uniform. She seemed to be answering questions. Her face was smudged with something—fatigue, or apprehension, or desolation. Shock probably most of all.

Their informant said, "They used to fly down once in a while for the weekend." He shook his head and went off, swinging his fish.

While Daniel put his postcard in the mail slot, Margaret heard a male voice saying, "It's a messy business," and a female one replying, "You can say that again."

Daniel and Margaret strolled down to the shore. When they came to a bench under a bit of thatch they sat on it, as mindlessly spontaneous as the two doves that lit on a nearby rock, Margaret thought. She returned to the images of the woman's face, last night's and this morning's. They blurred into one like the images of two lenses coming into focus.

The happy couple had been together when he died. She had tried to help him. She was now bereft. But she would have no place at his funeral. In his obituary there would be no mention of her. Whatever their love affair had been—Margaret turned away from conjectures and stood up. The startled doves' wings beat together in flight.

Halfway along the beach Daniel leaned down for something. It was a piece of white clam shell, broken and battered by waves and sand until it was only a small circle with a hole near the center. He took her left hand. "With this ring I thee wed," he promised, and pushed it on her finger above the old one made of tawdry platinum.

Carl Gustav Larus

The maturation of Carl Gustav Larus took some time. In his infancy, when he and two siblings remained near the nest of sticks and bones and feathers that his parents had arranged on the ground by an inland lake, he was fed from their beaks and sometimes sheltered from the sun by their bodies. If he wandered too far, strange gulls pecked his head and he hurried home. When he was led to nearby water, he swam by instinct. A little later he was impelled by an itching in his wings to stretch them, then to beat the air, and found that he was lifted from the land. Shortly thereafter he was on his own. His brown juvenile feathers were the mark of immaturity.

While he wore them, he learned the art of survival. His education came from doing, in the immemorial way of trial and error. Though the elemental act of flying had come to him from the egg, he had to perfect the skill. He had a few collisions in mid-air, many awkward landings, and numerous ignominious retreats from white-feathered adults. But the subtleties of flight were not hard to master—the rising, the falling, sideways plunges, foot-hanging droppings, swoops and turnings. Finally he got the hang of it all and could manage reverse flips and circlings no wider than his wing spread. This was trade school stuff, the polishing of basic technique. What was harder was to learn to outwit the competition, for the gull tribe was always present, and always hungry.

In his youth he often sat brooding, hunched on a rock or post, and wondered about the world. He knew, of course, that the Larus family was the center of it, was indeed the reason for which the world was made. Why else? At some time in flapping space it had been enunciated—the gull was supreme, and all other creatures subject to him.

This concept was beautiful and simple, but the working out of the

71

details was not. Though the world was full of goodies, they did not fall regularly into one's outstretched open beak. The Divine Egg from which all hatched had been bountiful. Indeed, She had been prodigal and imaginative in the extreme. But She had not made things easy. And since She could have, there must be some reason for Her refusal. Carl Gustav wondered why, in a world that was full of food, it was not always available.

After months of watching his elders in action, soaring and diving and scrambling, the existence of the Great Plan was revealed to him. This occurred just after he had taken a mussel from the very beak of an older bird, who had lifted it fresh from the knife of a fisherman and was flying away with a quark of triumph. As the succulent mollusk slid down Carl's gullet, the truth was manifested: the gull was supreme, but his supremacy had to be won. Each individual's survival proved his strength, his courage, and his cunning.

When hunger roused him, he dropped philosophy for action and took wing. The world he flew over was complicated and enriched by the presence of non-birds. Animals up to a certain size could be eaten alive; larger ones could be eaten after they were dead. Only the place of man in this scheme was ambiguous. Sometimes he spread food, sometimes he took it away. His mood was unpredictable. It was best to keep an eye on him.

At first Carl thought it was merely part of the seagull's luck to have a catholic taste. When he had put the facts of life together, he realized that his species was superior precisely because it was omnivorous. From the nest he had been used to an unrestricted diet. His parents had carried or vomited up for him whatever they had killed or fought over or scavenged for. He had dined on fresh crickets and dry bits of rat skin. He had fed on brine shrimp and flies, fruit and maggots, and young birds of all kinds, stolen from the nests of other birds. At Lucullan feasts his mother had brought in her mouth the eggs of ducks, which Carl and his siblings pecked open and slurped up. There was nothing that he would not, could not, did not, eat.

Carl Gustav had early noticed the variety of other feathered creatures. Then he noted that they were widely specialized. All were equipped for a particular act and diet. Herons with long legs and necks waded in still deep water, grabbing up a frog or fish. Pelicans dived in the ocean and surfaced with fish which they had to toss their heads to swallow. Cormorants flew faster and dived deeper. Some ducks dived and some dabbled. Gannets fell from heights one could not believe. Willets and sandpipers probed the shore with straight beaks. Curlews' beaks turned down. Godwits' beaks turned up. Spoonbills, oyster catchers, turnstones, egrets, each was equipped with some particular skill or structure. The tern, which looked like a gull of inferior size, was quick as the fall of drops of water. The hawk had an eye as sharp as doom. Only the magnificent frigate bird lived lordly on the work of others, and he could be outmaneuvered. The vulture, whose habits were sometimes embarrassingly familiar, could be ignored.

In contrast to all those creatures limited to a narrow life of repetition and a restricted diet, the gulls were almost free. When they could, they lived on the initial labor of others. When those others successfully defended what they had, the Larus family foraged and scavenged. By its wits and its willingness to eat anything, it survived.

When Carl Gustav became an adult, in glistening white plumage with grey primary coverts and mantle, and on his mandible a beautiful red spot symbolic of his source of power (it was thought to be a reminder of the yolk of the Great Egg) he traveled widely. His skill and confidence increased. He could grab a mussel or clam, fly high with it above the rocks, drop it and be down to claim his smashed tidbit before another gull arrived. He followed mergansers as they swam face downward in the shallows, and sometimes grabbed their catch. He had a favorite pelican, who tolerated him, and from whose bill he could pull bits of fish skin or an eye.

Sometimes he followed the farmer, feeding on worms and grubs the plow upturned. He followed the harvester, waiting for crickets and grasshoppers to be scattered. For this, man praised him. In one area, his kind was held sacred because it had destroyed a horde of crickets that had threatened man's survival. Tales were told of how the gulls had gorged, and vomited, and gorged again. A monument was raised to the bird. But when Carl swooped on the cherry crop, man's temper changed, and when he fed on young turkeys he was threatened. He followed the course of irrigation ditches and caught young mice. He lurked on school grounds and grabbed up castoffs. He devoured the smashed carcasses from highways. He rummaged in garbage dumps and sewage canals and harbors.

And always he grew in wisdom and cunning. He had passed the

time when he had been intimidated by his elders and backed away when one of them approached him as he pecked at a fish head. He had learned to stand his ground, and then to lord it over others. But among his peers there was always competition. Whenever he got something, the sky was suddenly filled with wings and cries. They materialized out of nowhere, full armed with envy. The gull with the booty had no chance to swallow it. He must soar, and turn, and dive, and jostle, and half the time lose his beakful to another, who in turn must struggle to escape. The battle was loud with calls of desperation and anguish. But part of it was fun. On a bright morning it was fine to chase and torment and outwit some miserable fellow carrying a piece of bread or a fish tail, especially if one was not really hungry. Afterward one could light on the water, and bathe one's feathers into shape, and float awhile.

If a boat with people in it came by, Carl Gustav followed it. For people also fished and caught things, and threw out guts or minnows. Men seemed to like to play, tossing stuff into the air for gulls to catch, laughing like gulls themselves at the scrambling and flopping. But sometimes there had been hazards. Once Carl seized a bit of bait from a trolling line, and half swallowed it, and was caught. The men in the boat wound him in, terrified into limpness, and cut out the hook. He escaped, and his wound healed, and he developed some suspicion which inhibited his instinct to swallow anything at all. He savored cigarette butts and bits of Kleenex instead of downing them thereafter.

The place of man in the scheme of things was never completely clear to Carl. Alternately ally and enemy, man could be neither scorned nor trusted. He was endured and used, as on the beach where the fishermen brought up their boats. Here was the market place, the jousting field, the bourse. Here pelicans and gulls waited each morning, quiet as stones. The knives of the fishermen flashed and slit. Then a boy would gather up a handful of bones and tails and guts and throw them on the shore.

Wings rose and slashed and threatened. Bills grabbed and missed and snatched. In a minute everything easy was gone. The unlucky walked away, hunched in dejection. The only action then was from the pelicans, struggling with a vertebra too large to be engulfed, a head with spines that prevented swallowing, or a string of skin and tail that would not slip down. Then occurred one of Carl Gustav's finest moments. Quickly he would drop to the pelican's side and grab whatever hung outside the great awkward beak. When the pelican opened his mouth in a retching effort to swallow, Carl would reach inside and pull off a morsel. His technique was versatile and opportunist. He sometimes sat on the pelican's head while his host gulped and gagged. He was ready for the moment of defeat when the pelican must give up his trophy, and the gulls would converge, pecking and pulling and dragging until nothing was left but a fleshless bone. Then they would walk off, to wait for the next incalculable harvest. Carl would sit on an empty boat, or discipline the immature birds to the sidelines, or make brief flights to see if there was action elsewhere.

At the appropriate time Carl flew far inland and with his mate hatched a clutch of mottled eggs. This period was too busy for reflection, but he had a gratifying sense of eternal recurrence when his young pipped through their shells. Periodically he moulted, grew feathers, preened himself. On the whole, he was content. The world had both diversity and sameness. Though food was more or less plentiful, the ocean was always full. And he, Carl Gustav, had reached the apex of his powers. By wits and wings he had survived. No one could ask for more. This large acceptance of life was his heritage. He knew it first in his brown feathers. And then, rising on white wings, supported by the air above the sea, he knew it in the small dark region behind his clever eyes. From the vast waters below came everything. Long ago the Original Egg had floated there, and hatched, and seagulls had flown up to range the world.

One noon he lazily rose over a peninsula and looked down on a quiet bay. There the surface was marked by a small commotion. At once he circled and peered closer. A sea lion was diving, surfacing, and diving. He was eating something. Carl dipped lower. The mammal was tearing up a fish with a yellow tail, caught in a tangle of twine. Carl lit on the water, watching. Then he made a quick foray above the sea lion's head, but the creature's teeth flashed at him. He watched the carving of the banquet from a distance. No crumbs came toward him. He rose and looked about and saw nearby another fish enmeshed and flashing. Carl's skill was on the water, not in the depths, but this fish was irresistible. Much smaller than the other, it was still a marvelous capture. Carl approached its flapping tail and went beneath the surface. Not like a loon or cormorant, but still with competence. His yellow bill caught the squirming fish, and he flapped to the air again. But when he lifted his wings to rise, he could not. Something held him. Though he writhed and struggled, he was caught.

The inevitable happened. From nowhere other gulls appeared. But they did not help him. One grabbed his fish, another took it and flew off. The whole tribe followed, screaming pursuit and conquest. Around the peninsula they vanished.

Carl Gustav strove alone. The sea lion idled past him, his round eyes serene and knowing. By late afternoon Carl was exhausted. He had managed only to complicate the net that held him. When two men in a boat came by, they swore at the mangled yellowtail the sea lion had mostly devoured. Then they looked at Carl, floating. Their wrath descended on him. Robber, they said. Thief. One grabbed him up and wrung his neck. He gave a diminishing squawk and fell limp in the water. His last thought was of survival in another world, where large filets of mackerel lay about him, interspersed with oysters already loosened from their shells.

The Smiling Angel

At two o'clock in the morning Laurie Pryne sat in a hospital room waiting for her husband to die. The room was lit by a small lamp in one corner, its shade tipped down like a modest eyelid. It ignored the bare neatness of the room, the small purposeful clutter of equipment on the bedside table, and Laurie herself. It ignored the thin body on the bed. But in the dusk she could see the outline of the man under the white coverlet, the quiet arms, and the profile of the face with the white beard, looking in its unmoving silence like a carved effigy on a tomb.

Laurie sat by the window in a rocking chair. "Don't you want to go home?" the night nurse had asked. "We can call you if there is any change."

"No, I'll stay awhile."

The nurse lingered in her duties. "You have such a pretty smile, Mrs. Pryne," she said.

"My husband always said that was why he married me, not because I had any virtues." They both laughed a little.

"How long have you been married?" The nurse was very young.

"Fifty years."

"That's a long time for a smile to last." Or anything, she was probably thinking. "Well, I'll be on the floor if you need me." But she came back in a few minutes with a pillow. "Rest your head on this."

From the window Laurie could see the city lights, fewer at this hour than when she had first looked in the early evening. Then the neon had been blood-red, and blue, and green, like the daubs of color on a palette. But as the hours went by, the bright colors faded, and now there were only lines of white, meaningless scrawls and sketches. She leaned her head against the back of the chair, on the pillow. She had already

77

gone through the dreadful first gate of widowhood—recognition that he soon must die, then disbelief, then pain. There had been moments of hope and denial. But that had been only the mind and the heart refusing to believe. Now both were beaten by the long hours at the bedside. Ever since Griffin had first looked at her she had been waiting. Now was not very different, except that she was old, and it was later at night than usual. She had merely come to the last waiting of all, for the doctor held out little hope. "We never know," he said kindly. But she knew. Griffin was eighty years old. She was seventy.

She looked at the narrow shape on the bed. She could see the mound of his forehead, his almost fleshless nose, his white beard. He had worn the beard ever since he went to Paris the first time, the first time she had begun her life of waiting. When he left, he had been clean-shaven, like all the other Kansas boys. He had come back with the full blond beard of the artist of those days. She remembered how strange it had seemed under the dark foreign hat. All her life she had been married to a beard, she thought, almost laughing. But silently, which was fortunate, for just then a nurse came in, quiet but not stealthy. "I've brought you a cup of coffee, Mrs. Pryne," she said. "Don't you want to lie down in the lounge off the hall?"

"That's nice of you," Laurie said. "You're all so kind to me. But I'll stay here awhile. And thank you for the coffee." The nurse looked carefully at the shape on the bed and went out. The coffee was black. She liked it sweet. Griffin had always scorned her for putting sugar in it. "Coffee should be strong and black and bitter, like life," he said. "Don't always be trying to sweeten things. Take them as they are. See them as they are." That was the artist speaking. All his life he had tried to paint things as they were. And she had waited. She drank the coffee like a duty, and then rose to put the cup on the table. Her husband's body was unmoving, but once in awhile a hoarse sound came from his throat. She went back to the rocking chair, the lights of the city, and her vigil.

They had lived in a small Kansas town at first, but it was no place for a painter, except of barns, he said bitterly. So they moved west, to an artists' colony on the coast. On the way, he changed his name from George to Griffin. She remembered the afternoon they had spent looking through a dictionary while tiresome flat scenery crawled past the train window. In the list of Common English Given Names was "George: A husbandman." Next morning at breakfast he said, "From now on you are going to be Mrs. Griffin Pryne." She stopped pouring cream and sugar in her coffee. "How do you like being married to a fabulous beast instead of to an ordinary mortal?"

"Wasn't there a Saint George who killed dragons?"

"I don't want to be named for a saint either," he said.

In the freedom of a new country and the inspiration of a new scene, Griffin found himself. But it took a long time. It took months of sitting on the cliff above the Pacific. For hours at a time he would sit, staring at sea and sun, until the sun was gone and the sea was almost black. Or he would climb the hills and stare at the clouds and the horizon, or walk on the shore, his feet almost in the waves. Out of all this he developed the Pryne style, a manner fresh in those days, of sparkling sunlight on water, and the tourists to the little town began to buy his pictures. They were hung in the shops, and in the local gallery. Eventually a big one hung in the bank above the president's desk. Griffin became famous, to the distance of several hundred miles. But this was not until the thick blond beard had become grey.

While Griffin worked and reworked, Laurie waited. She waited for the paintings to be finished, to be sold, to be admired and known. She waited to have children, but none came. She started writing little stories, poems, sketches. First she made them up while she was posing, to take her mind from her aching muscles. Then she wrote them down and submitted them to little magazines, church publications, and newspapers. They sold, not for much, but for something. Griffin was outraged. "It's hack work," he said. "You can't do this. It's prostitution." But his pictures weren't selling. He was in a difficult period before his brush had learned its craft. She continued, writing little tales of small-town life, and poems that jingled or sang a small melody, and human-interest notes for journals. But she wrote under her maiden name. There was really no need to be so careful. No one Griffin knew would have read them.

She half rose at the sound of a cough from the bed, but he was quiet before she got to her feet, leaning on the chair arm. His arms lay outside the covers, stretched out like the legs of an easel. She lowered herself to the chair and closed her eyes, her knees stiff, as if she had spent hours in posing.

When his pictures began to sell, Griffin bought a house with an adequate studio. He hired a model when he needed one. He took trips. He was fifty-five years old. People's attitude toward him changed. He was pointed out first with condescension, then with affectionate interest, finally with civic pride. He was asked to speak at exhibition openings at the Gallery, and later on even at meetings of the Women's Club. He sometimes accepted these invitations because, he said, it gave him a chance to tell people what was wrong with them. This widening fame led to visitors coming to the studio, some to buy, some to pay homage, some simply to snoop around to see if there was a nude model under the skylight, Griffin said. Laurie had to cope with them. It was not always easy. People with money in their pocket felt that they were privileged to go where they chose.

The problem of uninvited admirers was solved by having open house once a week. A friend made a tile with a griffin for the front wall. Laurie hung a small sign underneath, Visitors Sunday 3-6. At first Griffin objected. "We look like a damned institution," he said. But after a while he grew to like the affairs. There were usually not many callers, and most of these did not stay long. The ones who did remain were friends. Laurie served coffee and cake. The air got heavy with tobacco smoke, the clanging of pottery beads and silver bangles and dropped spoons, praise of present artists and condemnation of departed ones. Sometimes people stayed very late, and they would have wine and sandwiches. Griffin said whisky was no drink for artists.

She was rarely neglected on these Sundays. She knew that this was less because of her high-piled golden hair and soft grey eyes than for her willingness to listen. This had always been so, both when she was young and when her hair had silvered. In the early days, in the small studio walled with canvases, someone was always eager to tell of his projects, his pains, or his passions. Several painters made attempts to include her in the passion, with praise for the color of her skin, the tilt of her head, and other fleshly charms that Griffin had delineated on canvas but that they felt could be displayed better if she would pose for them. She declined, with the smile that closed the door without slamming it. Although Griffin said that the world of the artist could not be circumscribed or fettered, and found nothing to disapprove of in models who stepped from the platform to the couch, in regard to his wife he was a Kansas yokel. So Roberto the sculptor told them, the same one who remarked that it was a curious switch to have the griffin protected by the pot of gold. Thereafter he called her *dama d'oro*, with a look she appreciated but did not return.

These evenings had been pleasant, Laurie mused, though even then she had sometimes seemed to be waiting, but for what she did not know. Surely not only for the evening to end so that she could pick up the plates with ashes scattered over the cake crumbs, the cups and glasses with cigarette butts floating in the dregs, the pillows piled on the floor. It still seemed odd to her that artists, who were so fussy about the exact shape, the right color, the final polish on their work, who fumed when their pictures were hung without the best possible light or were framed imperfectly, were so careless in the way they lived. Griffin had explained it to her many times. Artists were concerned with what really mattered, not with the inessentials like dust on the floor and whether a stove was old or new.

Still, Griffin liked to have some order in his life. He spent hours trimming his beard. He liked shining window panes and well-cooked meals. For her the problem was to achieve these things. He hated noise, the swinging of doors, the banging of a broom, the calls of peddlers, the neighbor's radio or barking dog. Such things distracted and disturbed him. Odors too annoyed him, especially the homely smells of domestic life, ham and furniture polish and laundry soap. All these were enemies that invaded the world of the imagination where his life unfolded. She was constantly on guard against the interrupting sound or smell that might ruin a morning's work.

And the meals. Sometimes Griffin would work right through lunchtime. Sometimes he would stop early. Often he would return from a painting trip too exhausted to eat. Occasionally he would throw his paint rag into the air and shout, and when she came running he would pick her up and dance around the studio. And then he might say, "We've got to celebrate. Let's go to Breton's for lunch." And she would change her dress and turn out the fire under the soup kettle. "Hurry," he would say. And she would leave the house while still putting on her hat or pulling down her skirt. He was always saying, "Hurry. Don't you know that time is all we have in life? Don't waste it." At the restaurant, leaning on the red checked tablecloth, eating *pâté maison* and *coq au vin*, he would talk furiously. On the way home they would walk along the promenade, or sit on a boulder on the shore. Often they would stand or sit while the clouds piled high with color, and diminished, and the grey and black of night covered the sky, and the wind grew cold. She would rub her hands and wiggle her toes, while he stared at a world halfway between headland and horizon. As if time did not exist, or could be controlled, like the shapes of things.

Now she too was lost in her preoccupation, and did not hear the quiet opening of the door. "Mrs. Pryne?" the nurse said softly.

"Yes?" She was startled back to the bedside and the present.

"I thought you might be sleeping."

"No, just resting."

"Well, our patient is too. He seems the same. I'll check again in an hour," she said, and closed the door.

Laurie looked toward her husband. How many times she had seen him asleep, deep in a life of his own, regardless of the world, oblivious of her. He had always slept deeply, while she floated on the surface, awake to any sound or movement. "You should let yourself go," he said. "Just give in and sleep will come." But often it did not come, and she lay from owl cry to cock crow, waiting for the dawn and another day of small useful tasks and simple pleasures.

She remembered a depth of night when she had seen him by moonlight, asleep by her side in the wooden bed they had brought from Kansas. Her mother's blue and white quilt had been replaced by a Mexican serape. She had lain for a long time watching the quiet face, and the rise and fall of his chest. Once in a while his hand had clenched.

He had returned at night from a trip to New York where he had taken paintings to a dealer. It was spring, and she had cleaned the house while he was gone, airing things and polishing wood. In the evenings she had sewn by hand a nightgown of blue silk. This too was an activity she had done away from his eye. She had thought she could sew while he worked on her portrait, or made sketches of her feet or legs, but it distracted him. Even when one day he decided to paint her as she sewed she had had to hold the needle still, an artifice and falseness that spoiled the picture for her. She was glad when someone bought it.

Griffin stayed in New York a long time. She wandered around the overclean and quiet house, dawdled over the solitary and sketchy meals of the widow, made and received visits. She wrote a ballad and put it in the fire. One evening walking on the beach she met Roberto, who took her off to dinner, and over glasses of California wine threatened to take her off to Florence.

"I'd love to go," she said, playing with temptation and the wine glass.

"The Botticelli ladies have hair like yours," he said.

Her house was cold when they entered, with the damp chill of the seaside. She lighted a lamp, and turned to see Roberto, broad and dark as Griffin was tall and fair, watching her. When he reached for her hand, she felt her loneliness like a pain that must be soothed and comforted by flesh. His strong hands lifted her, enclosed her, in a warmth she had never felt. But before she melted utterly, as she was about to melt, she heard him saying, "You're as beautiful as a Leonardo angel." And she was frozen into the little girl from Kansas who had memorized all the Commandments, and now could not break one of them.

"You're a fool, you know," Roberto said. "Life is all we have. Don't waste it. Some day you'll be old, and regret will burn you like an acid."

"I can't. I can't." Something held her rigid, some armature of habit, of old principle, of fear.

"Don't think Griffin would be so faithful," he taunted. Then he bowed, and kissed her hand, and went away. She sat a long time in the cold bedroom, brushing her hair, brushing away desire, burnishing her self-esteem.

The night Griffin returned, she wore the blue silk nightgown. He didn't notice. He was tired from the long train-journey and the excitements of New York. "Good night," he said, and fell asleep.

Let yourself go. Life is all we have. You are a fool. It is too late. It is better to be a fallen angel than a neglected one. She lifted her hands above his sleeping head and could have brought them down on him. But as her fists shook there, silent, pale in the moonlight, the silent tears of misery and regret came burning, and she could not see the target of her rage.

On the back porch she crouched on the steps until the built-up climax of a sob relieved her. She wiped her eyes and blew her nose on the nightgown, took it off, and put it into the trash can. She went back to bed wearing an old cotton shift fit only for a paint rag.

After so many years, her shrivelled thighs still remembered their rejection. But she should have known. What innocence, to think that her golden hair would be enough. The first time Griffin took her walking, on a hot Sunday afternoon in Kansas when he still was George, she had worn white dimity with a blue silk belt. "You look like an angel," he said. "You sound like God praising one of his flock," she said, for even at seventeen she was not really stupid.

They had walked along a shady road where there were pigs in a field, a sow and her litter. Laurie had laughed, because she was a female and all young things drew her heart. Their skin—black, pink, whitish— was stretched tight over oval bodies. Their ears flapped. Their tails drooped, and then curled with excitement. They stood still, sniffing. For no reason, they darted, all in a frenzy, crowding and squealing. One flung himself under a bottom board of the fence, where he was wedged, and cried, hopeless and alone. Laurie laughed and could almost have cried too. But Griffin dropped her hand and started sketching pigs' snouts and legs and bellies, drawing over his lines in correction. When she spoke he did not answer. Even on the way home he stopped to change his drawings. "You seem to prefer pigs to me," she said, because she really was rather stupid.

She should have known. Instead, she had said yes when he asked her to wait for him, while he went to Paris to become an artist instead of a farmer. All girls said yes, when their hearts were touched. And lived happily ever after, some of them. She too. And yet—something had been missing. She had never said a sentence that anyone would remember.

Tomorrow she would begin to speak. She would say—but what? That it was too late? If one waited, it would always be too late?

It was too late now. Nothing of herself would remain. No child. No picture. Her casual little poems were gone like meals that had been eaten. She had never shaped the world. Her hands had washed cups, and never made them. Even the portraits of her were not she. Picture of a woman sewing. Picture of a girl in sunlight. Face under a pink umbrella. They had been painted by someone else, while she waited. A waiter. One who serves. A time server. Not a maker. Not even a maker of her own life. Not even a fallen angel. Just one of the cloudy multitude, the background mass with golden hair and acquiescent simpers, attendants upon the acts that shaped the world.

And now even Death was making her attend him. He loomed dark in the corner, silent and powerful. At any moment he could make the merciful gesture, throw his black cloak over the vanquished head. He could finish what must be done, kindly and quickly. But he took his time. Arrogant and self-centered, confident and calculating, he waited. For what? For the stage to be set, for the light to be just right, for the patient to move a little, the head to be turned or the hand twisted, so that the composition should be perfect, the color arresting, and the meaning revealed in all its horror or glory?

Before long he would be waiting for her, in that teasing, infuriating way. Laurie rose from the chair, holding to the arm with her left hand. The pillow slid downward and she bent to pick it up.

Griffin's face was a blank mask as she looked down on it, dark on the side toward her, the other lighted by the moonlight of the lamp. The white beard moved a little as the mouth opened and shut. What was it saying—Good-bye? Forgive me? I love you? The eyes opened and Laurie leaned toward them. But they were focused on a distance halfway between himself and the wall. He did not see the patient figure in the corner, or the patient figure by the bed. The eyelids closed, and a rasping gurgle shook the beard.

"No," said Laurie, "I've had enough." She lifted the pillow to the face and covered it, pressing hard against the bed. When she lifted the pillow the sound had stopped, all motion had stopped. The room was very empty, like a studio for rent. She sat again in the chair and put the pillow behind her head. Then she closed her eyes and waited, her lips twitched upward, almost in a smile.

The Spacious World
of Aunt Louise

Dazzled by sunshine, Catherine glanced into the dark well of the garbage can. Quickly she dumped a colander of eggshells, coffee grounds and rhubarb trimmings, and forced tight the misshapen lid. Stepping back from the lilac bush that shielded it, she smelled the fragrance of flowers mingled with the stench of the battered tin, outrageous and sickening. "We've got to get a new garbage can," she thought. "We've simply got to. I'm not going to put it off another week."

Her three-year-old daughter grabbed her knees. Her oldest was at kindergarten. Her youngest was sleeping. "Mamma!" said Sharon. "Postman put something in a box."

From the mailbox nailed to the front porch too high for the children to reach, Catherine lifted out a gas bill, a postcard notice of a Sunday School picnic, and a white envelope postmarked Chicago. She noted the amount of the bill and the date of the picnic, frowning against the sun.

"What cha got, mamma," said Sharon.

"A letter."

"What for?"

"I don't know." She sat with the envelope in one hand, the colander in the other, looking at the postmark.

"Is it a birthday, huh?" Sharon tugged her printed skirt, jiggling the flowers that were faded to a pale jumble.

"No," she laughed, and put the pan on the step beside her. On heavy paper was the simple statement that the will of Louise Lancaster, deceased, would be read at a place and time prescribed by law. But the words were so heavily legal and the style so ponderous that Catherine read it several times before she realized the meaning. Then she sat smelling lilacs and not listening to Sharon's repetitions.

Aunt Louise, she thought. Aunt Louise is dead. She felt a twitch at the corners of her mouth. Like a cold wave the thought of her own mortality first chilled and then warmed her. She was sitting on the unpainted porch, surrounded by her daughter's tugging questions and the lilacs of spring. She was not dead.

Aunt Louise was dead. The thought was a shock, beyond the shock of death itself. She had not seen her for many years, but Aunt Louise had been a recurring presence in her childhood. She had been real flesh and blood, but with the looming magnificence of a totem pole. The relationship was not that between Catherine and her other aunts, her father's sisters. For Aunt Louise was a great-aunt. And she was rich. Not merely well-to-do. She had a house with pillars and wide terraces and marble steps. A butler opened the door. There was always a smell of flowers.

About twice a year Catherine and her mother had gone to Aunt Louise's big white house for luncheon. There were always other remote relatives, cousins and in-laws, who met at no other time. They darted, floated, swooped, making polite noises and semiannual comments. "Why hello, Catherine! What a pretty little girl you've grown! And what a big girl!" Part of the excitement seemed to have been that no one except Aunt Louise ever spoke in sentences. The talk sprayed out like water from a sprinkler.

Catherine's stomach had always been filled with the wings of panic when her mother called the taxi to go to Aunt Louise's. Her hair hung in limp curls, her silk socks crept around her ankles, lint collected on the vaselined surface of her Mary Janes. Her hands were cold in their kid gloves. But she enjoyed the ride, sitting stiffly near the folds of her mother's silk dress. She enjoyed walking up the three marble steps to the entrance hall where a lamp hung from a chain. Once on a rainy day it had been lighted when they left, and she had watched it, like a star in the gloom as they went off down the drive.

In the house was an ecstasy of polished floors and sudden thick rugs where she delighted in the extravagance of change. Even her feet reveled in the speed and danger of parquetry, the luxuriance and ease of oriental depth. On all sides, windows full of light alternated with dark pictures of women in plumes and ruffles, haughty and assured, whose tireless eyes followed Catherine as she wandered, looking at the porcelain and filigree on the little tables, or staring at the great gold harp. It was the only one she had ever seen, except in the picture in the storybook about the giant who surprisingly played one. She longed to touch it, to run her fingers up and down the strings, not missing one. But she did not dare. One time Aunt Louise saw her looking at it, entranced and bug-eyed, and said, "Would you like to play the harp, Catherine?"

"Oh yes," she said, hoping to be allowed to touch it.

But Aunt Louise was lighting a cigarette. "You really should have this one," she puffed. "No one has played it since Carla Rosetti did a concert here last year."

"Catherine is taking piano lessons," said her mother.

"That's nice," said Aunt Louise. And then the butler said it was time for lunch.

At luncheon there were silver trays of carved and molded things cut out to resemble flowers and leaves, too pretty to eat, prodigal as dandelions. At home afterward she could never eat much dinner and her father would say, "Did you have too many peanuts at the circus?" and her mother would jerk her chin at him.

Sitting on the porch with Sharon at her side, Catherine thought of how she had at first accepted the paced and polished world of Aunt Louise as just another remarkable bright spot in the unnoteworthy year, like Christmas, and the masks of Halloween. Mechanically she smoothed Sharon's soft, fine hair, a movement like brushing away veils. Her own hair had been so, soft and straight and colorless. It had had to be wound around rags and tied into horrid bumps before parties and for Sundays. But that agony had magnified the change from her ordinary self, in blue gingham and braids, to the festive self in silk and curls. And the ordeal had taught her to wait, to sleep in discomfort, to be patient until morning.

There were rarely any other children at Aunt Louise's. She would have liked someone to discuss things with, like the butler's faraway expression and the incredible water closet in the powder room. But one day there had been a new third or fourth little cousin. She had been about Catherine's age, and had a halo of black ringlets irresistible to adult fingers. After luncheon the girls had obediently gone out to look at the rose gardens. The paths were gravel and curved in calculated complexity around roses of pink and crimson, white and yellow. First they had walked in prim silence, having no currency of conversation. Then Catherine had skipped, her gold locket with the chip of diamond in the center flopping on her chest. When she looked back over her shoulder the other little girl still followed, walking daintily. Shaking her lank curls Catherine abruptly left the walk and squeezed between two bushes to hide her nose deep in a soft red whorl. When she straightened her back the lace of her collar caught on a thorn. "Oh," she said, scurrying back to the path, guilt and shame pounding her, "I've torn my best dress."

The remote cousin looked at her collar. "Your best dress?" And then, "Maybe Stevens upstairs can fix it."

"Oh, it doesn't matter, really," Catherine had said, quickly, smoothing the collar with her hand. And it didn't. No one noticed but her mother, and she mended the lace so carefully when they got home that no one would have ever guessed. But Catherine herself had been snagged by a thorn so sharp and small she hardly knew she had been touched. The intuition came to her later with the spread and conviction of a panorama. Rich people don't have best dresses. Standing in their petticoats before the wardrobe door, they can make a choice. Which rose, a pink one or a yellow, or perhaps this white one, that looks so simple and naive, but is rarest of them all. Some day, she thought, I'll have a dozen party dresses, all different, with slippers to match, and I'll have a maid to curl my hair.

After that she still enjoyed the vasty stretch of the entrance hall, and looked forward to seeing the porcelain vases on either side of the drawing room. Perhaps she now liked them more than ever. They were Chinese, ornate and curved and very tall. The design was intricate and the glaze had a shine, a glow about it. But the most fascinating thing was that they were always filled with an extravagance of blossoms— rhododendrons or hydrangeas, Easter lilies or peach blossoms. She had often wondered, on the way in the taxi, what flowers would be there this time. The guessing had got to be part of the ritual of the visit. And although she had not mentioned it to anyone, one day when Aunt Louise said, down the length of the luncheon table, "What are you thinking, Catherine, you're so quiet," the fact popcorned out of her hot confusion before she knew it, and everybody laughed and said how charming. Aunt Louise laughed too and said, "I didn't know anyone but me ever noticed them particularly."

A little later Catherine's parents moved to a distant western city, and she never saw her great-aunt again. Gradually the family ties, held by habit and proximity, frayed and broke. Catherine grew into a soft round girl with undistinguished legs and an attractive smile. Her blue eyes were eager and she read Sara Teasdale and filled a hope chest with linen and silk things. She was married young to a nice boy named Lester who loved her. He worked in a store and planned some day to have a shop of his own. "We won't have much at first," he said, "but in a few years I'll be able to give you everything."

"I know you will," she said.

Aunt Louise sent them a wedding present of a silver coffee service. Catherine kept it on the low table in the living room the first year of their life together in the small brick cottage. When Sylvia started crawling it had to be put up on the sideboard. Then when Sharon stole the sugar tongs and used them to pull angleworms out of the garden, Catherine put the whole thing, tray and all, in the closet. It tarnished quickly anyway, not being used. And especially after Sally was born there really wasn't room for it in the crowded little house.

There was always an overflow. On the front porch were milk bottles waiting to be brought in or taken away. On the back porch were galoshes, a kiddie car with a wobbly front wheel, and a baby buggy. Every chair seemed to have a doll on it, or a block. The overstuffed sofa filled one wall of the living room. The crystal water goblets, and matching iced tea and sherbet glasses, all etched with a star design, were on the top shelf. When Catherine got them out for birthday dinners she had to wash them before they were used, and never relaxed until they were put back. In the kitchen the enamel sterilizer was always full of bottles waiting to be boiled or filled. In the bedroom the sewing basket was never empty.

Lester had done better in the store, but not well enough to start a business. At first they had expected to save, penny by hopeful penny, but always they seemed to have to spend, dollar by dollar. It would take longer than they had thought.

On summer evenings when the children were asleep Catherine and Lester sat in the front yard, and she felt the world expand as darkness covered the details of houses and trees. Lester's warm hand held her to the present, but she sometimes thought of the uncluttered world of her childhood, so far away now that only by fixing on some star of the first magnitude could she be sure it had existed. Among other things she remembered the great entrance hall of Aunt Louise's. Their whole house would fit into that spacious room. She thought of it now, holding the letter from Chicago, and Aunt Louise against the doorway, dressed with the stark simplicity made possible by a million dollars. But Aunt Louise was dead as any housewife. Dead and buried, and her will was to be read. And with this recognition Catherine admitted the question she had ignored as she drowsed in reminiscence and warm sunshine. How much had Aunt Louise left her? For surely she had been left something, or why this notice? Still, she had really no claim. The relationship was remote. And there were all those others. But if there was nothing, why should they tell her?

What would it be—a hundred dollars? Two or three? Perhaps a thousand? It couldn't possibly be less. Aunt Louise would never have bothered with less. Sharon leaned against her knee. Catherine clasped her. She would buy white shoes for all the children, and a blue lace dress, and she and Lester would go to the lake and leave the children with a nurse, and—she bounced to her feet and swung Sharon around by her arms. "Isn't it a wonderful day! Feel the sunshine, smell the lilacs, Oh Sharon!" Turning to go inside, she saw the coffee-splattered colander. "And a new garbage can. That first of all. This very day."

In the cool of the house she slowly put the colander in the sink. A few coffee grounds stuck to her fingers and one long pale tendril of rhubarb coiled around her thumb. She peeled it off and rinsed her hands. No, she said to the water tap. I won't tell anyone. I'll wait till it comes.

She hid the letter in her bureau drawer, under her rayon slips and stockings. She flipped them back in. I'll buy new ones, she thought. White ones. Nylon. Silk maybe. She buried the news in her breast, where it burned so hot she had to take an extra breath every little while to cool it off. It was like being pregnant, happy and weighted with a burden she wanted to be free of and yet keep forever.

Lester and the children didn't notice. They ate, and splashed water in the bathroom, and spread the newspapers around. They expected brown gravy and bread and jelly, and kisses on bumped elbows and cheerful hello dears. They attacked each day with innocent interest, having no thought of anything different, for better or for worse. She was almost disappointed. Alternately she scrubbed harder and let go entirely, thinking of the changes she would make. A thousand dollars was a lot of money. But it could hardly be less. It might even—but caution slapped a hand on her. Don't go counting your chickens. You're not going to Europe. You're just going to the lake. She didn't even buy the garbage can. That could wait. An heiress can put up with things. You don't mind doing without if you don't have to, she thought. That's a funny thing.

The reason came over her one evening when she was reading about Cinderella to the little girls. You don't mind troubles if there is to be an end of them. The children were touched by Cinderella's rags. They were delighted by the pumpkin and the mice. But most of all they sighed over the fairy godmother, and Catherine sensed their relief. Now there could be an escape from cruelty and cinders. A beautiful fairy had come whose golden touch would make possible the life of forever after. She had known it too as a child, the almost belief that somewhere there is someone who may pop up and wave a wand. Later she had dreamed more directly of the prince, but the older dream had been of the fairy godmother herself. In the vagueness of her fantasy, perhaps she had confused her with Aunt Louise, whose wand was a pen. But she had been right. The dreams of youth might seem silly to the old, the middle-aged, the stupid, but they did come true.

The day the will was to be read she made the children play quietly in their room, though the sun was shining. She brushed her hair for twenty minutes, thinking Aunt Louise is dead.

She heard nothing from Chicago for several days, for several aeons. She must be wrong. There was to be nothing. She stood at the window, looking at the lilacs on which the lavender had turned to brown. A spider let itself down from the roof on its thread, slowly, toward what impossible goal? Will he run out of silk, she thought, like a bobbin emptying before the end of the seam? She shook her head, and thought of writing to the lawyer. But it must take time to make out all those checks. It would be all right. They knew her address. How did they know her address. Aunt Louise must have kept track of her, even after the presents and greeting cards stopped coming. And all the other heirs, the second cousins and great-aunts she hadn't seen in years. Or thought of. Were they looking into a dark and empty mailbox too?

Thinking of them, she was carried again to Aunt Louise's, where her Mary Janes slid on the polished floors, and lace covered the polished table. The crystal that had held her water had been so shining she almost feared to touch it, like a blown bubble iridescent with light. The silver trays were rubbed to a dazzle. She thought guiltily of the coffee service, darkening in the closet. Aunt Louise's eyes seemed turned on her.

Climbing onto a chair, she lifted it down. The pot, the pitcher, the sugar bowl, were greyed. The big tray was like pewter, no, like lead. She carried them to the kitchen and rubbed with frenzy. Sharon and Sylvia came to see. She gave them little rags and they scrubbed too, with giggles, missing places. While she burnished, Catherine thought, We oughtn't to put things away. We ought to use them. When we get a bigger house we'll use them every night. We'll have coffee after dinner before the fireplace. Her hand fell to her side. The children would be sleeping, or off dancing in pink taffeta dresses, and she and Lester would sit in a room with soft lights, holding little cups. They would talk about things, and plan the vistas of the future, and she would laugh, shaking her head so that her rhinestone earrings would shine in the firelight.

When at last the tray was finished, she stood back to look. Sharon's and Sylvia's eyes glowed and for once they were silent, holding their pasty rags. It did look beautiful. She carried it in to the low table. In the small dark room it shone like a headlight in a tunnel. Impatiently, she turned away. Surely it was the thought of things stored away and useless that bothered her. She grew scornful of buried treasure, miserly hoards, dreams that mouldered, dank as unused linen. She felt a need to air things and plunged into trunks and bureaus.

She put Sally in a white dress that had been rolled in tissue paper. Sylvia had worn it, and then Sharon, but only for best. What was she saving it for? If there was another baby—but surely there wouldn't be— she'd buy new ones. She stood the baby up. The fine linen, the tucks, the insertion, made the practical black laced shoes look clumsy. The white ones would be nicer.

When Lester came home from work and found everything flopping on the line, sprawling on the grass, he said, "For gosh sakes, what's the matter with you?" She smiled, feeling like the Saturday before Easter. "It looks like you're moving. You aren't leaving me?" He pulled a piece of her hair that was hanging over her forehead.

Then the dam burst. The pot boiled over. Catherine couldn't stand it another minute. "Maybe I am," she said. "You too. All of us. Wait till you hear."

"Hear what." He looked like a man who was used to the ups and downs of a life with females. She would show him.

"I'm an heiress."

"You're crazy." He looked as if he half believed she was.

"No, really. I am. I will be. Aunt Louise has left me something." How stupid men are. How good and kind and stupid.

"Holy smoke. How much?" She was pleased to see him stagger, reconsider, apologize for his disbelief. She stood enjoying the sight, waving an old scarf back and forth. "How do you know?"

She had to tell him all then, sitting on the bumpy back lawn and supper not started. "Well I'll be," said Lester. "Do you suppose there'll be enough—" But he didn't finish. It was her money.

After the children were in bed they sat in the front yard, thinking. Catherine put her head on Lester's shoulder. Things she had never said, because they would hurt him, ached to come out. "Wouldn't it be nice," she said, "to—"

"To what?"

"Oh, just not to have to worry any more, ever. About anything." It was pleasant not to be too definite. She knew Lester couldn't afford to be so carefree. Men had to think, not dream. Even in the delivery room, when she had gone off in whiffs of nitrous oxide, leaving the bloated world of pain, Lester had been waiting, cold sober, planning for another small pink mouth that would be hungry, hungry, hungry. "I love you," she said.

"I love you too." She could feel him yawning against her cheek. "It's late," he said. It was Wednesday night. Half a working week was gone. There were three more days till Sunday.

On Saturday morning she washed her hair after Lester left for work and before she even cleared away the breakfast things. She had just rolled up the last back curl in a metal tube when the doorbell rang. On the narrow front porch was a man from the American Express Agency. "Mrs. Catherine Martin?" he asked. "Sign here."

She wrote her name with his indelible pencil. Mrs. Catherine Martin. That's me. The man watched her. She felt his eyes on the metal curlers.

"Where do you want them?" He repossessed his pencil.

"Well—I don't know." On the porch were two big boxes. "I guess in here." She half opened the door. "Are you sure they're for me?"

"Sure I'm sure. Never made a mistake," he said, and pushed inside, off balance with his burden. Sylvia and Sharon came screaming from the back yard. Sally cried at being left, and Catherine had to go to comfort her. She held the baby against the cold excited place in her breast, and felt her heart beating, like a stranger knocking. The little girls' cries of insistence dragged her to the house. The express truck was gone, and the two boxes filled most of the living room. Sylvia and Sharon hopped like sand fleas.

Catherine found the hammer and pried open a wooden top. Excelsior sprang up. The children pawed it. She lifted armloads from the box, dry, dusty and endless. At last her fingers touched a cold hard shape. Leaning into the darkness she lifted out one of Aunt Louise's vases and set it on the floor. "Ooh," said the little girls, their hands against their cheeks.

It was as tall as Sylvia, and much rounder. It was gold, and pink, and green, on a background of eggshell white. The design was intricate and rich. There were hills and houses, warriors and maidens. Ladies lifted their delicate hands, that were made for a gesture, eternal and useless, standing on little bridges made of bricks, or jewels. Men rode on short fat horses, or carried banners. And over all was a panoply of flowers, and small winding rivers, and dwarf trees with perfect fruit that could not be eaten.

Sally crawled over and patted its side. "No, no," Catherine said, "mustn't touch." But why not? She herself had longed to touch its surface, had put her fists behind her, when she was no taller than Sylvia, and ordinary rooms were large, and Aunt Louise's cavernous, and the summer sky a fearful blackness. Still she said, "No, no," and knelt to hold the baby. Her eyes came close to the vase. She was surprised to see that there were slight irregularities on its surface. Some of the color was worn off, and the faces were blurred. Sitting on her heels she realized that this was the first time she had ever really seen it. It had been surrounded before by the shapeless glow and glitter that was Aunt Louise's, and the soft amorphous hope of childhood. It had been a point to focus on, something bright and constant in a shifting strangeness. And always it had been filled with flowers, opulent and fragrant.

She ran her hand over her forehead and felt the tight pull of hair curlers. I suppose, she thought, they might be sold. But I don't suppose they're worth much. The little girls rolled over and over in the excelsior, that crackled like dry leaves.

She stood up, leaning against the unopened box. The inside of the vase was deep as a well. She knew it would echo if she called into it.

Ah Love, Remember Felis

When a woman wears a hat it is assumed, quite rightly, that she has
a destination or a project in the head under the hat. One might guess the
kind by observing the nature of the hat. So Beth Gilman thought, lifting hers from a shelf in her closet. It was a classic, low crowned, broad
brimmed, of natural straw, quite unadorned. No ribbon or flower distracted it from its function. It stayed on in the wind and shaded her eyes.
Suitable for a female of seven or seventy, for before the age of coyness or
after. Admirable. Unadmired. Cherished. Like a long-accustomed wife.

She put it on her head and went out of her house and got into her
car. She had already kissed her husband good-bye. If she were a different kind of woman she would put an artificial rose on the brim, or
tie a scarf around the crown. If she were a different woman she wouldn't
be going on this trip today. The thought occupied her for several miles
until she turned up a canyon road. By this time she had finished with the
hat. It sat on her head as easily as it had thirty years before when her hair
was brown.

As the road up the canyon grew steeper, Beth thrust the car smooth-
ly down into second gear. There was a time when the old sedan took
these curves with never a gasp or wheeze. It ran swiftly past anything she
wanted to pass. Now its age was showing. Hers too. The hands on the
steering wheel were misshappen. There were brown spots on the backs,
small marks of mileage like the dents on the car's fenders. However—
she shifted back to third—they were both still going. With the thought
came a warm wave of affection for the car, her servant and companion
all these years. Her feeling for it had been aroused first by the word horse
power, which she took literally, and saw hooves and a white mane. Under
the white hood was an animal sensibility. She said that there was an

empathy between them. Well, there had been Bucephalus. And Pegasus. She did not mind a slightly imperfect analogy.

Her husband had laughed at all that. In the days when he laughed much. This September morning Bart was at home in his wheelchair. The practical nurse would know what to do for a stroke victim. Beth thought of other strokes, of intuition or good luck. Now for her the word would always mean a jab of evil.

Still, he was alive, if unable to take this anniversary trip with her. She had not told him where she was going. If he did not understand, there would be no point. If he did, he might be saddened. She turned off the main canyon road into a flat place full of bright aspens and dark conifers. She did not have to think of where she was going. The car probably knew which parking place to go to. This had been a family joke too. So much of family life was silliness, which had a strength to support that one wouldn't believe, in one's unobservant youth.

The desired familiar spot was empty, a good omen, as if she was expected, would have been missed if she hadn't come. Not that she had to justify the trip. It was no rendezvous with a conspirator or lover. In fact, it was almost a pilgrimage, a journey one made for one's salvation. For absolution. For redemption. She shook her head. For a pagan, this was presumptuous. Highfalutin. All she had come for was to pick some berries.

She locked the car and carrying her basket walked down a narrow path toward the plunging stream. The gold and glisten of autumn shone on mountain slopes and granite outcrops. The path was dusty with the feet of summer. It led to a camp site on a small cliff above the water. She put her basket on a table by a chokecherry bush and sat on the bench to look around. It was the first time she had ever been here alone.

She and Bart had camped at this spot long ago on a day like this. After picking the service berries that hung dark purple on high bushes along the stream, they pitched a small tent, and cooked supper on a hot fire of squaw wood, the dead or downed branches of old trees. Even though they had collected it together, she had felt the term to be somewhat demeaning—wood that a squaw would pick up, not what a brave would chop with great brawny arms. She had not known, then, how strong a squaw could be.

Her awareness, her resentment, of the vulgar putdowns of gender no longer bothered her. This was a relief, like ceasing to ovulate. She had more important things to think about than why the sun was he, the moon

98

was she. She was concerned now with the earth and its survival. The sensible part of her brain gave a twitch and reminded her that she always thought of Mother Nature, or Mother Earth. If she ever thought of him, it was of Father Nature off somewhere flexing his muscles, planning earthquakes and other rapes of the land. A squirrel had climbed a pine tree and sat protesting something. Her perhaps. He was probably not commenting on the tall monolith across the stream, which antedated Freud and all passing nomenclature. Small private joke, for the moment unsharable. Ah well.

She looked around to where their tent had been, a low shelter beside aspens. There had been a storm in the night, quite unforeseeable, which woke them with a gigantic bang. Then there was lightning, flickers and slashes, mumblings and growlings, and reverberations that circled the canyon walls. There was no escape, the car was too far away. For distraction, for comic relief in the drama, they spoke of Zeus commanding his full orchestra, exhorting the tympani to greater efforts. This made him less ferocious, funnier. But the lightning was a real hazard, and when the sky lit up around them as if to reveal the explosion of the world, they drew together. Surrounded by the inhuman threat of thunder, the almost-human groaning of the wind in the pines, they had mingled fears and bodies.

Sitting in the lonely sunshine she thought of that night of noise and mingling. If Zeus was directing this small human scene in the intervals of thunder claps, the scenario was quite to be expected. The great Thunderer was also the great Philanderer, lover of whatever his hot eye fell upon. A role model for mankind.

No bolt had struck them and when the rain stopped they slept. Next morning they spread things to dry on bushes, and walked in a freshened world. On two logs they crossed the stream, a precarious trip for her, but he had held her hand. They went into a meadow of yellowing grass and purple asters and then to a bare place under pines. When she looked down she saw big paw prints in the still wet ground. More than big—enormous. What dog was this, she said. Bart bent down too, and then they looked at each other. The paw marks had no claws.

Had he been holed up somewhere, not too far away, during the storm, and come out when the rain had stopped, to prowl under the now bright stars? Felis concolor he was. Older and more formidable than Zeus. Even now she sometimes looked down for paw prints on the dampened earth.

She tucked two paper sacks in her pants pockets and carrying a third walked along a path above the stream. There were a few bushes with berries but the crop was poor. She knew a better place and went on, through a tangle of stalks and vines, the dogwood's useless white berries, a few late pink roses, crimson rowan berries. An unknown fragrance came to her at times, one she had never been able to identify, to attach to anything. It hung in the air like a teasing promise, coy and tantalizing, like youth's hope that the world would be full of riches. The scent was delicious and frustrating. She liked to have a name for things.

When she reached a great granite boulder by the stream she looked around. At the top of the rock, rooted in the steep cliff above the water, was a spreading bush with a wealth of purple berries. At its base were a few new plants with a scanty crop. She considered, but no, she could not crawl up the rock to reach the bounty at the peak.

"Damn," she said aloud. "Triple damn." Silently she cursed her knees and indifferent fate. Another stroke of bad luck. Once Bart would have made a run and leaped up, and then pulled her to the top. They would have filled their bags, eating a few squashed berries that tasted a little like strange raisins, winelike. Now, thwarted, grounded, she started picking what was within reach. There would be a few. She felt no resignation in her.

While she searched she heard footsteps, human of course, and a male voice said, "Hi!" The universal greeting.

"Hi!" she said, not looking around.

"What are you picking?" It was a frequent question. Her answer depended on how she was feeling. To children she usually said, "Service berries," and smiled, unless they had been chasing around whacking the heads from the monkshoods. If she was really irked, had seen them throwing cans in the stream, she sometimes growled, "Death berries," and waved her blue fingers at them. She hoped they thought her a witch as they retreated, a crone gathering something poisonous for a darksome brew. Sometimes she was bored with herself. Once she had been tempted to direct a tobacco-chewing pair with tatoos on their chests to the shiney white dogwood berries. "Moon berries," she wanted to hiss. "They will make you more than a man." She would leer and cackle. But she couldn't quite manage it. It remained a phantasy for the future. Bart would have been shocked. There are things a wife can't do. There are a lot of things she can't tell a husband.

Today she said, "Service berries." The young man had curly hair. No beard, thank God. She was tired of beards that made them all look alike. Jeans and a T-shirt of course. He had a big back pack. After a few minutes he put it down.

"There are a lot up there," he said, pointing.

"I know," she said, answering his silly statement politely.

"What do you do with them?"

"I make jelly."

She could see him walk back a few feet, crouch slightly, spring up the rock, and then crawl to the top. How easy it looked. If one had the knees of twenty summers. She went on gleaning. He took off his T-shirt and tied the bottom in a knot and started picking. His bare back and arms moved fluently as he reached. She felt a stab of envy and then a hot flash of anger. He was a trespasser, a competitor, an enemy. This was her land, her harvest, by reason of seniority. He intruded on a private act. Arrogant and careless youth. A creature of flowing muscles and endless breath. He had no idea what it was like to live in a wheelchair.

Once she would have been up there, hot in the sunshine, her fingers blue and sticky, laughing. Part of the unhappiness of being alone was that there was no one to laugh with. Only witches laugh to themselves, eerily, evilly.

She had finished gleaning but her sack was less than half full. She would have to search somewhere else. She looked up at the young man. His arms were busy, holding down a branch and stripping the fruit. And her anger was stopped by admiration, for efficiency had always pleased her. There was a beauty in it. More than beauty. A rightness. Something lasting. Beauty was transient, like youth. Watching him, her eyes performed a camera trick and sped up his life before her. She saw the lithe arms thinned and stringy, the quick hands slowed, the blond hair whitened. And felt a stroke of grief, for Bart, for herself, and for the boy. Her bag was pitifully light in her hand, but she did not begrudge him his picking. This was his time to collect the fruits of the world, while he could. She had had hers.

She was turning away when he slid down the boulder, holding his shirt in a bunch in one fist. It was stained and bulging. "Gee," he said, smiling, "I got quite a lot. What'll we do with them?"

"We?" she asked.

"Well sure. They're for you. For your jelly."

She remembered how she had accused him of theft, in her selfish mind, before she had given them to him as his right. There was a wonderful kind of justice in his giving them back to her now. It was a matter of grace, to give and to accept. "Thank you," she said.

"Do you have another sack?"

Carefully they filled two bags. He shook out his shirt and put it on, stained with purple juice.

"Your shirt is ruined," she said. "I'm sorry."

"It doesn't matter. I'm just going up into the wilderness."

"Where?"

"To the top of the canyon. I'm going to stay overnight."

"By yourself?"

"Yes."

"Then first you must share my lunch."

"Thanks." He had the grace to accept. "Thank you very much."

She led him along the narrow path. Why had she made two thick sandwiches, brought a quart of coffee. Partly it was habit, and the poignancy of bringing only one where always there had been two was bitter. And she was a Westerner and never went far from home without provisions. One never knew what might happen outside the providence of the town. A breakdown. A washout. An unexpected guest. Back at the picnic table she said, "This is a chokecherry bush. They make jelly too but I prefer the service berries." He looked up, interested.

"I'm going to tell my wife about them," he said as they sat down across from each other.

"You're married?" It didn't seem possible, he was so young. Perhaps he meant it for the future.

"I'm going to be next week. I'm twenty-four." He must have read her mind.

"I'm very happy for you." She handed him a roast beef sandwich.

"I'm going up the canyon by myself for a last fling with solitude, to sort of think things over and put my life in order. Afterwards, after next week, things won't be the same."

She could have been flippant. You don't know the half of it, Bub. You're telling me? But he wasn't the sort who throws beer cans in the stream. "No," she said. "It will never be the same again. Life, I mean. Yours and hers. But it will be together. Not just in what people call conjugal bliss. But sharing things like walking and laughing and picking berries." Simple things that seem so everlasting, but are not. She could not tell him that.

"Is your husband alive?" He saw her ring and her wrinkles.

"Yes. He has had a stroke. He lives in a wheelchair."

"I'm sorry." But the idea was not quite credible to him, here in the September sunshine, by the sound of running water. It hardly was to her.

"We used to come here every year. It was a kind of pagan ceremony near the autumn equinox." They sat eating for a time. Elemental food. Bread and meat. "One of the things that keep marriage alive is the little ritual that has meaning for us, that we make ourselves."

"I'll remember that. And will you tell Sally how to make the jelly?"

"Gladly." Jelly making was still the female's job. Her province. Her mystery. She filled the enamel cup with coffee for him, and poured hers into the thermos top. "Once several years ago we were sitting here drinking coffee and looking at the stream, and a mink came down on the other bank, very slow, looking around, and stood at the edge of the water. He had a chipmunk in his mouth. He stayed a long time. I always see him here."

"That's great." He turned around, looking at the far bank. She wished she could evoke a dark slim mink for him. She would have to be more than a witch.

"What will you do after you are married?" She put bananas and pecan cookies on the table.

"Sally teaches in elementary school. I work for the county assessor. Maybe if I get smart enough I'll go into politics."

"And improve the world?"

"I hope so. It's pretty rotten you know."

"I know." You're telling me?

"But just now I have to think about my own life. Mine and Sally's. How it will be. That's why I'm going up to the mountain. It's kind of frightening, you know, to promise to love, honor, and cherish somebody for the rest of your life. Even if you want to and mean to, how can you be sure? How can you know that what is drawing you together now will keep you together forever?"

"You can't know. You can only try to keep it going." The squirrel was back, scolding. "Shut up, Squirrel! What do you know about forever?" She was stalling for time, waiting for a stroke of knowledge.

"What kept your marriage going?"

What indeed? Habit. Inertia. Memories. Duty. A few small rituals. She could say this to a contemporary, but not to him. Not now. "Perhaps a poet said it best. 'Ah, love, let us be true to one another.' Perhaps he meant let us be true to what we had in the beginning."

"I'll think about that tonight up on the mountain."

It was not enough. She wanted to say more. "Before you go I must tell you about Felis concolor." She told him about the night of the thunder and rain, and of the big cat padding softly, stealthily, alien, unknowable, on the margin of their ignorance.

He was quiet for awhile and then he said, "That's great. That's really great."

Had she said enough? "If you are not faithful the memory will stalk you always, like a lion in the night."

"We plan to be."

"I know."

He collected the wax paper and banana peels and put them in the litter can. "Now I know Felis concolor's name and I'll watch out for him. But I don't know yours." They wrote their names and addresses on pieces of paper sacks. "Beth," he read. "Is it all right if I call you by your first name?"

"Of course, Clark." They bowed very formally and laughed together. What a pleasant sound it was, in the hot stillness and the little rippling clapping of aspen leaves.

"Thank you for the lunch," he said.

"Thank you for the berries." She watched him slip into his pack.

"Well." Partings were awkward. "Good luck with the jelly."

"I'll send Sally the recipe."

He grinned and took off. After a few steps he turned and waved. "Good-bye, Beth," he called. His curls gleamed gold in a stroke of sunlight before he passed into the shade.

"Good-bye." There was only the sound of stream and aspens. Nothing human but herself, though the initials of other humanoids hoping for more than mortality had been carved in the tree trunks. She took off her hat and sat awhile in the cooling afternoon, and thought of Clark going up the mountain, slowly because of the heavy pack. It would be a clear night. Big stars would shine on his struggle with incertitude. Perhaps a star would fall, an omen, a stroke of inhuman light that would confirm his hope. It was more than she could give him.

She put her admirable and cherished hat back on her head and slowly walked up the steep little path to the parking place. For an instant she had an image of an old horse waiting, head down, patient and reliable, whose power would take her where she needed to go. The sight was a comfort. She unlocked the car and put the basket on the seat. Then she patted the white metal flank before she got inside.

There was no one to see, or wonder, or laugh at her, an old woman going off with a picking of simples to make a brew to preserve her from the teeth and claws of time.

The World of Borg

When Professor Herbert Borg met Vyella Langer on the steps of the library one autumn afternoon, he did not know at once who she was. The wives of instructors tended to look very similar, like minor Elizabethan lyrics or the wails of contemporary poetasters. He looked downward, trying to remember. He was returning a volume with an error in the epigraph to "Lycidas" which he intended to point out to the librarian. Vyella was carrying away a volume of Anne Sexton and she held it out to him, "Do you think names are significant for a poet?" she asked.

"Quite possibly," he replied. "Though I don't believe it would be safe to make any inference about the name of Milton."

It was an odd comment, but she smiled. "I'll tell Bob I saw you. He's so fond of you." And then he remembered who she was.

That evening Vyella told her husband that Professor Borg had spent some time looking down at her legs. She had known at once who he was.

He was almost as much a part of the campus as the carillon, rather large and imposing, taken for granted, and occasionally listened to. His older colleagues had grown used to him and were aware of his virtues. Human repositories of the past have value, if only because they save a trip to the archives. Borg knew a lot of things, and sometimes when smashing new ideas came up he could demolish them, for reasons A to Z documented in something published in 1895, before someone rushed into print and made a spectacle of himself.

The younger members of the English department, untenured and on tenterhooks, were aware of him as a presence whose name might be run across in obscure journals. His physical presence was noticeable when it was noticed. For them to see Professor Borg on a winter day, but-

toned in overcoat, jacket, vest, shirt (and undershirt probably) was to
realize how far we have come. And Mrs. Borg, stuffed into who knows
what chemises and petticoats and girdles. Clothes obviously inhibit one,
insulate one from the vital flow of things. If nature is good, and clearly
it is, and man and woman (currently persons) are a part of nature (nat-
urally), it follows that one should live close to the source and get on with
it. This fashionable syllogism had no discernible flaw. In a lilting coda
Vyella opined that if Professor Borg ever got Mrs. Borg undone he would
probably be undone with the effort. No wonder they had no children.

Some of the older members of the department drifted toward an
appearance of modernity in turtlenecks and plaid slacks. The youngest
of both sexes wore shorts, or jeans, or skirts up to the thigh, their hair
flowing in all directions and their language flowing even looser. They did
their thing to the tempo and tune of today. In contrast, the Borgs lived
(This is living? The question did come up.) fixed in the modes and mores
of a remote past. They were anachronisms. Relicts. Vestigial fragments.
Antedeluvian hangovers. Pre-Freudian leftovers. You name it. But the
Borgs seemed as unaware of their difference as rocks against which
waves splashed.

Professor Borg's specialty was the seventeenth century, a small area
of the past as irrelevant to today as his tightly buttoned vest. Of course
everyone revered Shakespeare and Spenser, and *To His Coy Mistress* still
was effective persuasion for getting somebody into the sack. But it had
been a stilted period, no doubt about it. Everyone agreed, sitting around
in patched Levi's and T-shirts and beads, that nothing is as funny as a
discarded fashion. And that the Kiss and Remember school of literature
had been supplanted by the Piss and Tell.

Even so, it was sometimes admitted that Herbert Borg's old-fashioned and unhurried manner was rather attractive to anyone who wanted
to unburden himself of a problem, or do a little off the cuff (cuff?—off
the loincloth) ranting. But it caused him to get honked at a lot at traffic lights, and frowned at during faculty meetings when he elucidated
small, obscure, and overlooked items tangential to the agenda. He had
no sense of the urgency of time, of the need to get things done. What
things? he would ask, and cause a further small delay. It was taken for
granted (a shaky major premise, he was prone to remind all and every)
that he was illiberal, being elderly. He harked to the past. He was not
with it. And never had been. He seemed to live in a world filled with

slow crawling dragons and ladies draped in stiff brocade.

Actually he lived in a house built in 1903, surrounded by heavy carved furniture and fabrics of wool or silk, some of them mended. Shelves were crammed with his books and Mrs. Borg's bibelots—vases and figurines and objects of no discernible function but to collect dust and amazed glances. The pictures on the walls were oils or watercolors. There wasn't a Mondrian or an African mask in the place. Drinks were never served in plastic containers.

To this slow-paced, untimely world the Borgs invited the young occasionally to dine. These parties were something of an ordeal to the guests, who felt like new chicks in an ornithologist's study, and were glad to fly off after gorging themselves on Bertilda Borg's schnitzels and Linzer torte. But they did often have a rather snobbish feeling that they had glimpsed for an evening the wings of the passenger pigeon or the eye of the dodo.

When Bob and Vyella Langer received an invitation to dine with the Borgs on an evening in October, Vyella at least was not fazed. The other guests might be considering the length of their skirts or their sentences, but not she. She had skin like white rose petals down to her navel and up to her buttocks, and this delicacy of dermis and a durability of ego was a combination that had never failed her. Besides, she rather liked the Borgs. Her grandparents had looked like that. They had talked funny too. But not the same way.

Professor Borg's speech tended to be polysyllabic, except when he enunciated some of the four letter words of his interest—life, love, hate, envy, song, wind, rain, and star. Of certain four letter words that echoed in the corridors and evacuated onto the printed page, "You think you discovered them?" he would ask. "Vulgarians in the Neolithic spoke them." He would go on with his discourse, sometimes pausing, searching for the right word. When he found it, frequently no one knew what it meant, but he would explain. Though slow, he was impressive. His monologue never petered out in shrugs, or "You get what I mean," or "That's the general idea." He was willing to wait, to risk the hazard that his sentence might fail because the end was too far from the beginning or the danger that his audience might walk away.

Bertilda spoke much less. Vyella, identifying her with the grandmother who was usually in the kitchen, knew that women did not express themselves back then. She did not know that Bertilda had walked carrying banners, had written letters. Once when a Famous Writer had come to the campus to give a talk, afterwards he had kissed Bertilda's hand, and walked off with his arms around the shoulders of both Borgs, much to the chagrin of the faculty who had anticipated an evening warm in the reflected glory of the great, and had even done some homework. But that was before Vyella's time.

When Herbert came home on the evening of the dinner party, he was greeted with the faint rich aroma of his wife's cooking and the slightly sharp note of her voice. "You are late!" He was frequently late, but not on Fridays.

"I know. I stopped at the bookstore."

"Not today?"

"Today. Obviously." His voice too was a bit sharp. "Who's coming to dinner?"

"The Langers. The Weavers. The Solbermans." He put a book on the table by the hall and started toward the stairs. "Take your book with you."

"No. Don't touch it. I want it there." She was too preoccupied with the sauce in the kitchen to argue.

At seven o'clock their guests were received by Herbert wearing his second best suit and a benign expression. Bertilda was in a long, black velvet skirt and a tight, red, buttoned jacket. The effect was so old-fashioned that it was almost fashionable, almost ethnic even, Vyella thought, watching her hostess passing crackers and an unknown pâté. She had seated herself under a lamplight that caressed her long blonde hair. They were drinking sherry of an unknown vintner. The Borgs never offered a choice of drink. They served what they apparently deemed appropriate. It was hard to tell if this custom was parochial or cosmopolitan. The sherry seemed to go with the dark, warm living room.

"This never came from California," said Fits Weaver, accepting more.

"No," said Herbert. "It crossed the sea from its homeland." And the evening was launched.

The forebodings of the guests had been unnecessary. At the dinner table there were some ideas interlarded like the *boeuf en daube* with bits of gossip. Some crisp greens of comment. Though Bob Langer paraphrased two paragraphs from his thesis on existentialism, and Vyella described at some length her frustration while waiting for Godot to come, there had been no protracted and sodden memories of academic fiascoes. When the strudel was finished there was a little pause like that at the end of a semester.

"That was a really gourmet repast," said Vyella. The Borgs glanced at each other.

"In the vernacular, a great feast," said Fits Weaver.

"Just what does gourmet mean anyway?" asked his wife Lily, who had sudden inexplicable urges to deflate Vyella's balloon.

Vyella stared back. "It means—*au courant.* Sophisticated. Creative."

"Like putting lingonberries in the rice pudding and flaming it with gin?" asked Jan Solberman, joining forces with Lily. They were both brunettes.

Bertilda rose. "I fear my cuisine is not very innovative. I stay with the classics."

The word followed them back to the living room, where two of the walls were filled with bookshelves. The books were mainly dark and old. Nothing after 1900 apparently. Well yes. *The Magic Mountain* and *A la Recherche du Temps Perdu.* One ought to be fair, thought Solberman. He brought his attention back to his host who was standing before the fireplace and Langer, who was saying, "Well, Milton is a problem now, since nobody believes in heaven and hell any longer."

"Heaven and hell have always been metaphors," said Herbert. "They are eternal. The world according to Jehovah . . ." He paused, frowning over the *mot juste.*

Vyella looked up at him and crossed her legs. She had been counting the tiny buttons down the front of Bertilda's red bodice. Twenty. Incredible. She could get dressed from the skin out in the time it took Bertilda to do up all those. "What do you think of *The World According To Garp,* Professor Borg?"

He turned toward her, making a slow journey of some centuries. "According to whom?"

"Garp," she replied, as if the word were as familiar as the zipper.

"It's a novel," said Bertilda. "You wouldn't have heard of it."

"A philosophical novel?" asked Herbert. "The world according to some scheme?"

"In a way," said Weaver. "It's an account of Garp's progress through the world of lust."

"Is this Garp a literary descendant of Pilgrim?"

They all laughed merrily, even Bertilda. But it was sometimes hard to tell if Herbert's innocence was a put-on.

"Garp and Pilgrim aren't exactly using the same language," said Weaver, "though some of Garp's goes back a long way."

"Then I deduce," said Herbert, "that the lust is pelvic."

"As in a lot of classics," said Solberman.

"The thing about Garp," said Vyella, crossing her legs the other way, "is he's open to all kinds of experiences. He rushes into everything. He knows life's too short to fool around with . . ." She almost said buttons.

"To fool around with verses and virgins, when he could be busy with Volvos and vulvas." Solberman sounded a trifle grim, as if his witticism had taken something out of him.

Bertilda appeared quite unperturbed. One of the dark volumes on the shelves was by Huysmans. "We must all make choices and hope they are the right ones." Lily and Jan glanced at each other. Of course she had long ago made all the interesting ones. And age thinks it is privileged to be banal.

Herbert stepped to the little table by the hall door and picked up the book he had put there. "I assume, on the basis of previous experience with the species, that Garp believes he has made some discoveries in the world of lust. I would read to him some lines from a predecessor, John Donne, who was made popular for a time by a passing innovator, one Ernest Hemingway, who had revelations of a pelvic nature in a sleeping bag." He had found his page. "This is called 'Going to Bed'."

> *Come Madam, come, all rest my*
> *powers defie,*
> *Until I labour, I in labour lie.*
> *The foe oft-times having the foe in*
> *sight,*
> *Is tir'd with standing though he*
> *never fight.*
> *Off with that girdle, like heavens*
> *zone glittering,*
> *But a far fairer world incompassing.*
> *Unpin that spangled breastplate*
> *which you wear,*
> *That th'eyes of busie fooles may be*
> *stopt there.*
> *Unlace your self, for that harmonious*
> *chyme,*

> *Tells me from you, that now it is*
> *bed time.*

He closed the book. "What follows is more specific. Quite modern. You will no doubt want to look it up."

He had a sense of form all right, old Herbert. His guests rose as if at the ringing of a bell. Thanks and handshakes and compliments mingled at the door.

Outside, the guests paused for a minute by their cars. "That was rather nice," said Lily, "but why do you suppose they asked us?"

"They probably want to keep in touch with the young," said Weaver. "They want to still be with it."

"We're where the action is, I guess," said Jan.

"It's kind of sad," said Solberman. "Elegiac somehow. But that sherry was the real thing."

"I think Professor Borg gets turned on by us," giggled Vyella. "We start his glands flowing."

"Let's get the gasoline flowing," said Langer. It was his longest sentence in some time. At home he undressed in silence.

"If they invite us again shall I accept?" asked Vyella, unzipping her dress and stepping out of it in one motion.

"They won't ask us," said her husband, "so the question is academic."

She was so used to hearing the word in a variety of obscure connections that she dropped the subject along with her panty hose.

"I'm going right to sleep," he said. "I've got a headache."

Herbert helped Bertilda put away a few things and poked down the fire. He picked up the Donne volume and stood looking at it. "Is that the book you bought today?" Bertilda asked. "I thought you had one."

"This is the one. I gave it to Langer a couple of years ago because I thought a solid old volume would improve his perspective on things. Today—I found it in the used book section."

"Will you never learn?" She shook her head. "You have no mandate from a celestial board of regents to improve the world!"

He shrugged. "I may have taught him something about honor."

"In the world according to Herbert the impossible is always possible." She turned out the lamp.

He took her arm. "Let's go to bed." They climbed the stairs, help-ing or impeding each other. At the landing he said, "I always liked that jacket. All those little buttons. But my fingers used to be quicker."

"They're quite quick enough," she said. "It's your head that isn't."

Grandpa Pigeon

Jaclyn Kay rarely hurried on the way home from anywhere except when it was cold and her bare legs got goosebumps. Then she tripped along, hugging her arms to her chest. It was a little warmer at home, but not much.

The gas stove heated the kitchen and they kept the door into the rest of the house closed. There was plenty of room for Jaclyn, who was eight, and her sister Marilyn, who was two years older, and their mother who was ageless. When her father lived with them the place was more crowded. He moved around in the house a lot when he wasn't working. Even when he sat sprawled looking at the TV he used a great deal of room. His talk about what was wrong with the world took up a lot of space.

He had been loudly angry at the way the country was run. When he got out of the army, and there weren't any jobs, he said over and over how They were responsible for the mess the world was in, and the poverty, and the lack of work. They were in City Hall and Washington and the Pentagon, and God damn it in the pulpit too if the truth were known. They ought to be kicked out. If anybody had half a ball They would be. Jaclyn had no idea who They were and was afraid to ask. A bunch of gangsters, her father said. She felt uneasy away from home after nightfall. If she ever hurried it was then.

The house was very empty when her father left. One day he just went away and took the TV with him.

Life got more monotonous for Jaclyn. She missed his talk about how the world was screwed up. Her mother sat around a lot not saying anything. She was always getting up at night to see if the doors were locked. Marilyn sat around reading comic books or making cross-stitches on the ends of old tea towels. Marilyn was a round blonde cheerful girl who liked to sleep. Jaclyn was slim and dark and hated to stay long in any one place. But after dark she didn't want to go outdoors. Some of Them from City Hall might be waiting around.

While school lasted Jaclyn had no real problems. It wasn't much fun but it was something to do. Things happened. She ate the lunch that everyone did whether they paid or not. Sometimes she traded with another girl: She got two plates of meat loaf and potatoes and gravy, and her friend got two pieces of cake. But during vacation summer stretched hot and empty forever. Her mother gave up looking for a job. Whatever welfare was, they lived on it. They all gave up hoping father would come back and bring the TV with him.

The girls went to the public library on afternoons when the Story Lady gave readings. She was very dramatic and opened her eyes wide or narrowed them in suspicion, and shrieked or whispered at appropriate moments. Marilyn would stay on afterwards to read, but Jaclyn wandered along the streets, looking in windows at clothes and toys and bicycles. She stared at the movie theatre where a long time ago her parents had taken her and Marilyn. She had forgotten the films. What she remembered was the popcorn, a big bag full of crunchy puffs thickly buttered, that diminished and ended with the picture and remained an oily taste in her mouth. She stood by the entrance looking at episodes of coming events and smelling the fragrance. She lingered outside Benny's Grill, where a man in a white cap fried hamburgers and an aroma of meat and grease came through the door. She smelled it still at supper time, eating beans or vegetable soup or mush.

They sometimes played a game called What Would You Have To Eat If You Could Have Anything You Wanted. Marilyn always chose chocolate cake or doughnuts or butterscotch sundae. Their mother had grown up on a farm and thought of thick cream and green peas and peaches. But Jaclyn longed always for meat—pork chops and meat loaf and ham.

Their father had started it one evening when he was talking about being in the war. The men had been fighting in the field for several days, separated from supplies, and had eaten all their rations. Then the battle had eased, and a supply wagon appeared. All it had was oatmeal, but it was plentiful and hot. He had sat eating it, slowly, tasting it, his helmeted head bent forward to keep the rain out. "That was the best damn meal I ever had." Then their mother had started crying.

Later the parents remembered other meals, some of them shared—steak and chow mein and crab à la king. Jaclyn got the impression that They eat that sort of stuff all the time. Lobsters too. And caviar, which sounded nasty.

In summer Jaclyn often went to a little park not far from her home. There wasn't much to do there either, but there were trees and circles planted with stiff red flowers in the middle and yellow stiff ones around the edge. Pigeons walked on the paths making bubbling sounds from their fat chests. People sat on the benches and fed them. Jaclyn only watched. Some were very tame and came close to people's feet.

One oldish man was very good at bringing them to his hand. Patiently he held it out low to the ground, not moving, and making a few little bubbling sounds. The pigeons would walk close on their funny inturned pink toes, and wait. They would come nearer, their heads bent to one side. They would look at the man's hand with one eye tipped toward him. Then a bird would come close and peck. Others would come. There would be a flurry of white wings and a great scramble for food. It was all very lively and pretty.

One day the man had a bag of popcorn. "Do you want to feed them some?" he asked Jaclyn, holding out the sack. She took a few grains and threw them. The man offered her some more. Afterwards her hands were greasy and she licked them slowly, down to the fingertips. "You have some, too," the man said, holding out the bag. She hesitated and took a handful.

"Thank you. I love popcorn." She ate slowly. She didn't want to seem as greedy as a pigeon.

The man was very friendly. He was older than her father. He was quiet and asked quiet casual questions about her parents and what was her name and how she liked school and stuff. Next time she saw him in the park he was feeding peanuts to the pigeons. She accepted a few and asked him if he was a grandpa to anybody. "No," he said, "I'm not so fortunate. Maybe I can be your grandpa in the park." Jaclyn smiled and accepted a few more peanuts.

"What's your name?" she asked.

"You can call me Grandpa. But don't tell anyone. They'd know I'm only a pretend grandfather and laugh at us."

"Yes," Jaclyn agreed. She knew how people are. "I can call you Grandpa Pigeon."

Next day the oldish man had two hot dogs in buns in a bag. "I thought maybe the birds needed some meat in their diet," he said, "but they don't seem to like it. We'd better eat them." He handed one to Jaclyn.

"Maybe they don't like mustard," she said. "But I do."

"What else do you like?"

"Oh—" She chewed dreamily, making the hot dog last. "Fried chicken. And ham. And meat balls."

"Do you like steak?"

"I can't remember exactly. I think so."

The man fed part of his bun to the pigeons. "That was almost like a picnic. We ought to have a picnic someday." But then he suddenly stood up. "Gotta go now. See you later." He walked away, not really hurrying.

Jaclyn looked back when a woman with a baby carriage stopped before her. "Do you know that man?" she asked. Jaclyn was surprised, because she sounded almost like her mother.

"Yes," she said.

"What's his name?"

"Grandpa Pigeon," said Jaclyn, glad to have an answer.

"Well—" said the woman, and then went off pushing her baby carriage. Once she stopped and looked back.

Next day the old man had only a small bag of wheat for the pigeons. He and Jaclyn scattered it carelessly. He talked about the picnic. They would have it in his back yard under the trees. "We'll have steak, a great big thick juicy piece of sirloin. We'll cook it on a bed of coals until it gets all brown outside, and turn it over and cook the other side. Then we'll put on some salt and a big piece of butter, and slice into it. The middle will be just pink, the best steak anybody ever put his teeth in. Ummm." He licked his lips. Jaclyn licked hers.

"When?" she asked.

"Can you come tomorrow?"

"I think so. Yes."

"Now don't tell anybody. We don't want to have to share that great big beautiful steak with anybody who wouldn't appreciate it." She knew about sharing. It meant smaller pieces.

All afternoon she thought of the picnic. She ate her macaroni supper without tasting a thing. She washed the dishes without protest. Afterwards she could hardly sleep for thinking of the steak, the crusty brownness, the pink inside running with juice.

When she got to the park she was out of breath from hurrying. There had been no problem about coming. Her mother was away baby-sitting for a neighbor. Marilyn was off somewhere. But it had taken her a little time to pin over the waist of one of Marilyn's outgrown shorts. They were bright pink and seemed right for a picnic. She sat on the bench and waited. The pigeons walked around, waiting. After awhile they flew off to a woman who was tossing pieces of bread. The woman with the baby carriage came and sat down. "Hello," she said. The baby was awake. Jaclyn watched it waving its hands and pulling up its legs and smiling. "Do you like babies?" the woman asked.

"Yes." Actually she didn't know much about babies. Her father had said anybody who brought babies into this filthy world ought to have their head examined. But you did, said her mother. I was crazy, he said.

The baby was very pretty and Jaclyn looked at it when she wasn't watching for the old man. "Are you waiting for somebody?" asked the woman.

"Yes."

"Your Grandpa Pigeon?"

"Yes."

"Why doesn't he meet you at your house?"

That was a hard one. She thought a minute. "It's nicer here. The flowers and all. We don't have some at home."

"Oh." The woman looked at her watch. "We have to go now. Do you want to walk along with us? We might meet him."

"No. I said I'd be here. He wouldn't like it."

Sitting on the hot bench, getting thirstier and hungrier, she tried to figure things out. Maybe the old man had died. Maybe he had been teasing her all along. Maybe he was like her father, and just got tired and went away. Finally an explanation occurred to her. He was one of Them. He came from City Hall or Washington or someplace, and promised people stuff and made them think they'd get it. He was all a big bluff like the rest of Them. Now she would never, never in all her life have a big brown steak full of pink juice. She clenched her teeth on emptiness, to keep from crying at her loss.

But then from behind the bench the old man appeared. "Hello there," he smiled. "I'm late. I had to get things ready. Let's go out this way." He led her under the bushes that made a hedge along the street. "You didn't tell anybody about our picnic did you?"

"Oh no. It was a secret."

"That's a good girl." He glanced around and then hurried to a car by the curbing. "Hop in."

He was a very fast driver. He's probably hungry too, Jaclyn thought. After a short time he turned into a driveway. "Here we are," he said. "Hop out." He took her hand and walked toward the front door. The house was surrounded by a growth of dusty shrubbery that almost covered the windows.

"Aren't we going in the back yard," Jaclyn asked, "for the picnic?"

"We have to go inside first to get it. It's all waiting for you."

They entered a shadowy bare hall that seemed to stretch hugely toward the rear of the house. She heard the door click behind her, and the lock turn. Grandpa Pigeon looked down at her with a quite new expression on his familiar face.

The Convergence of Gerda

Every morning as regular as sunrise, Gerda braided her blonde hair and arranged it in a coil about her head. At sixty-five, her blondeness fading, she looked rather quaint in fashionable La Jolla. But her coiffure had reassured her landlady, Mrs. Le Grande, who had had experience of single women with mammoth hairdos stiff as a beehive; they did not pay their rent.

Mrs. Le Grande had not hesitated to ask Gerda about herself when she came to look at the one-room apartment on the top floor. Mrs. Le Grande glanced at Gerda's varicose veins and bumpy hands and asked if she was on welfare.

"No indeed," said Gerda, "I have an income," and she looked at the opal ring on her little finger. Miss Helena Hopkins, her deceased employer, had bequeathed it to her, along with two thousand dollars.

Mrs. Le Grande pointed out that the view from the window made up for the lack of a bath. There was a community tub down the hall. But there was a private toilet, and a double electric plate for cooking in an alcove.

Gerda paid a month's rent and began a life of her own. For the first time since she left her father's farm in Illinois, she was responsible only to herself. All the years she had cooked and ironed and polished for Miss Helena, her life had been filled with her employer's possessions and conceptions.

The Hopkins family had always been strong on saving. They looked down on people who lived on their capital. They criticized people who squandered. Miss Helena had never squandered much on salaries.

Coming of hard-working and frugal Dutch ancestry, Gerda had put a little away. It was too little to produce an income she could live on. But a rising tide of black and brown workers was flooding the kitchens and nurseries, and she would have to make it last as long as she could. So she figured and planned, and went toward a narrowing future that was like looking through a tunnel.

On this perspective was superimposed the view from her little room, through a gable window above a sloping roof, facing directly west. This window became the center of Gerda's life. From the table where she ate her meals she could see a stretch of sea. Sailboats or navy ships sometimes passed. At night small lights moved and stopped mysteriously.

By divine chance or the builder's calculation, the view from the window covered almost exactly the movement of the sun from north to south and back again as the year changed. When Gerda recognized this after her first year, she was filled with awe. At home on the farm she had learned only that sun and rain are necessary for a harvest. During all the time she had been keeping Miss Helena clean and tidy she had had no opportunity to think about the cosmos. In retirement she discovered an unimagined freedom. She began to perceive a connection in things. The progress of the sun, so dependable, so beautiful, gave proof that there was order in the world. She sensed at once that this order related even to her.

Every fine evening she stood at the window and watched the sun enter the water. This disappearance took only about three minutes. But sometimes the atmosphere did strange things to the perfect sun. It was stretched and moulded into amazing shapes of urns and pots and lanterns, then melted away. Sometimes the whole sky shouted with color for an hour. Other times the sun slipped into the grey sea without a murmur.

After sunset she ate dinner. She sometimes thought of the bread of her childhood when a loaf felt solid in the hand and smelled of sunshine. After her meal she drank a small glass of sherry. On days of fog or rain this warmed her. She went early to bed. There she told herself the events of the day, with comments, and listened until she became drowsy. She never went out at night. Old ladies had their purses snatched even on Girard Avenue.

She had become accustomed to taking a little wine with Miss Helena. When there were no friends in, and there was nothing interesting on television, Miss Helena dispensed wisdom and advice to Gerda, and they would sip Amontillado. Now Gerda bought a California sherry. Her budget was arranged to allow a half-gallon bottle a month. That was sixty-four ounces. Sixty-four ounces allowed two ounces a day for a thirty-one-day month, with two ounces over. In a thirty-day month, there were four ounces over. She saved this surplus for rainy evenings. The plan worked out well for February.

After Gerda moved into her apartment, Mrs. Le Grande asked out-and-out if she had social security. "No," said Gerda. "I wasn't publicly employed."

"But didn't your employer pay any social security for you?"

"Oh no. Miss Helena wouldn't have anything to do with socialism."

Mrs. Le Grande looked impressed. She took up where Miss Helena left off. As a property owner she had strong convictions. She deplored the condition of things in general and prophesied that they would get worse. Take taxes and prices, which were much too high. Take rents, which were much too low. Take morals, which were even lower. She sometimes felt that if everybody would go back where they came from things would improve. This embarrassed Gerda. On other days Mrs. Le Grande considered going home to Arkansas. But it was a bad time to sell.

The only people it was a good time for were the ones on relief. California had always been the promised land. First it was gold. Now it was welfare. People came from all over just to settle down and let others support them. And they had no sense of shame. It used to be if somebody was a pauper they went to the poor house. Everybody knew about it. Now they lived just like anybody else. Even better. Mrs. Le Grande had seen with her own eyes a woman on welfare buying filets of beef. Beer too.

When the time came that she could not pay her rent, Gerda did not know what she would do. Being on welfare was even worse than being on the streets. Though sinful, those poor women at least gave something. Reliefers just sat on their fat fannies and took. "Parasites," said Mrs. Le Grande. Gerda thought about it when she woke in the grey morning.

She had a large wardrobe of Miss Helena's castoffs, much too large and too fine to wear, of maroon velvet, black satin, blue crepe and lace. They enveloped her like the world of privilege she had looked on when she served tea to guests. She cut them down to her size. Sitting in the public library wearing a lavender beaded blouse, she felt a little overdressed, but at least she was not dowdy. From some of the leftover material of the dresses (the fabrics were always the finest) she made patchwork pillows and pincushions. She sold a few of these to a shop that specialized in quaintness and oddities. Buyers snatched up everything from Bibles bound in pink snakeskin to Wedgwood chamber pots. The selling point was novelty and Gerda's careful stitches had little market.

She spent a good deal of time at the library, especially after she discovered the art books. She concentrated on the Dutch masters and felt a kinship not only with the painters but with the subjects. When she saw Vermeer's painting of a girl pouring milk she recognized her, perhaps her mother or her aunt. People must have appreciated a clean strong working woman then, for an artist to have painted her. There were other homely scenes, orderly and recognizable. The world looked very solid, well-fed and peaceful. She looked long at the portraits of Frans Hals, so gay and healthy. She looked at the face of Rembrandt, who was neither, but seemed to know something beyond laughter.

When she got to van Gogh she remembered that Miss Helena had dismissed him as mad when people began talking about him many years before. Miss Helena had been very violent in denouncement. Gerda wondered what had made him mad and looked long at his centrifugal flowers and whirling suns. On the way home she stared at zinnias, at dahlias. The marigolds were whirls of light. At neat doorways she saw Vincent's tortured cypresses crying for help. Through her window that evening, she saw the sun looking fierier than before.

She remarked on this next day to Mrs. Le Grande. "Red sky at night, sailor's delight," said Mrs. Le Grande with authority. "Though I don't see any delight for anybody else. I just got my assessment. It looks like I'll have to raise my rents." Gerda looked at her toes. She felt as if the surgeon was already raising his knife. She could not survive this injury.

That afternoon, as she sat on the cliff staring hopelessly at the sea, she saw seven black blobs approaching the shore. When they got into the shallows they rose from the water and she could see that they were men, encased in black all over, with glass protuberances on their eyes and orange tanks on their backs. They walked up the shore backward, dragging their great flapping feet that were like a devil's or a demon's. Gerda thought vaguely of men from Mars. There had been much talk of interstellar space. She had heard that the money from taxes went largely to protect the country from invaders from far places. Perhaps this was what was meant. She hardly cared. When the creatures removed their tanks and stripped off their black costumes, they were revealed as ordinary-looking boys. But probably they were not.

In bed that night she thought for a long time of her diminishing money, that was being eaten away like the beach in a storm. Next day as she walked to the library she passed the food shop Miss Helena had patronized. In baskets were displayed the beauties of orchard and garden. Great clubs of asparagus, a dollar and ninety-nine cents a pound. Black figs on grape leaves, ninety-nine cents a pound. They must have come from Venus, or from Mars.

That was the day Gerda found the book of Hieronymus Bosch. She entered a new, yet a familiar world.

All afternoon she looked at demons and monsters. At first she almost laughed, they were so absurd: no one could believe in them. All afternoon she squinted and rubbed her eyes. There was a dog with a tree for a tail, and a bird sat in the tree. There were fishes with the heads of men, fishes like boats, fishes that flew. Men had the heads of rats, the feet of lizards, and pigs' snouts. Birds big as a cow had teeth and thorny tails. A green lizard breathed red flames. In every space lurked rodents, their whiskers twitching, their eyes gleaming. Skeletons and devils mingled with men.

And everywhere was cruelty and horror. Men were slashed and mangled, and impaled on trees and swords. One was being shod like a horse. One fried in a pan like a pork chop. One drowned in a tub. These scenes were too dreadful to believe in. But they were true. Or prophecy. When she went home the creatures accompanied her. She saw them on the street and felt them walking. They never left her again.

She could not tell when the knowledge came. It had been building up in her mind. First it was a vague feeling, very dawnlike. It grew stronger. During this period she felt uneasy, waiting for confirmation. Then it came with the splendor of full sunrise—the knowledge that the world would end.

She realized then that there had been intimations. She had wakened one night to the bang of thunder and lay watching lightning cross the sky. This display was rare in a region more used to the roaring of motorcycles and the spasms of neon. It took her back to her childhood, when only the very poor went in ragged clothes or walked barefoot. Now half the population wore no shoes. She felt that such poverty spoke of grave calamity. This message was not clear. But later it was hinted by the figures walking along the beach, men with long hair and beards, moving their arms as if preaching to the waves. The waves were full of rumors and shouts of disaster.

She could not walk on the beach in quiet any more. There were lewd pictures on the sea walls and words which no one scrubbed away. There was a stench of raw sewage which drained from pipes onto the shore. Almost naked men and women walked there, their long hair hiding their faces, but not in shame. Often one could not tell what sex they were. On the sand they sprawled together kissing, their legs and arms entwined, clutching at each other. They drank beer and tossed the cans over their shoulders, or sat smoking, crosslegged and stupefied. Some of them even said Hi to her, grinning and leering out of their beards. But the dogs were the worst. No one paid any attention to the placards that forbade them. Huge beasts ran loose, barking. Saint Bernards and Great Danes did their business everywhere. One could not avoid heaps of excrement and swarming flies.

A brown monster almost knocked her down on a path, and then returned to sniff her shopping bag where she had some liver and two cinnamon buns. The high prices were part of the horror. Thirty cents for a slice of liver, and ten cents apiece for yesterday's rolls. It was not believable. Everyone said so. Mrs. Le Grande asked what the world was coming to, all this inflation and high taxes and all. Gerda knew what it was coming to. It was coming to an end.

She made plans, waiting for a signal. She knew the direction it would come from.

First there were flights of birds going south. They flew in great numbers, low over the water or far up in the sky, in V shapes or straight lines. They flew away from the eroded cliffs; away from the girls with strings of cloth over their private parts; away from the men encased in rubber, carrying spears; the barking, defecating dogs. They left the miasma of the tainted land. They knew what was coming and wrote a warning in the sky.

The final revelation came after sunset of a bright blue day. Wind had blown away the smog. The sky was darkening. A new moon was following the sun's path. Suddenly there was a line of light coming from low over the horizon. It rose quickly, grew brighter, and shaped into zigzags that covered a large expanse of sky. Then the head of the movement exploded, and a great green mass hung in the darkness, speaking of terror and beauty to come.

But when? The message remained in the sky a long time, irregular and complex. Gerda had time to translate it. The numbers eleven and three could be discerned. On November third the end would come.

After dinner Gerda drank a full glass of wine. There was no need to ration it any longer. She relaxed as after long travail or reprieve.

Mrs. Le Grande said a missile had exploded, a catastrophe costing millions of dollars. "Such a loss."

"There is more to come," said Gerda.

November second was clear and sunny. Gerda walked slowly along Girard Avenue to the food shop. She had already reconnoitered. At the meat counter she purchased a filet mignon; the price was wicked. Then she chose three stalks of mammoth asparagus. She paused between strawberries and figs and chose the berries. She loitered by the wine. When she decided on a rosé de cabernet, the clerk smiled. "You'll enjoy this, Madam. It's fit for a special occasion." Gerda looked sharply at him, but his face revealed only a clerk's compliance.

Her second stop was at the library to say goodbye to Hieronymus Bosch. *The Garden of Terrestrial Delights* smiled at her. Pale people strolled in naked innocence. They bathed in blue pools and caressed one another. The animals walked demurely. Everywhere were berries, big as a man. There was no end to the delights, nor to the space and order of the scene.

Standing at her window at precisely six o'clock (She had ignored the return to Standard Time) Gerda watched as the sun touched the sea. She could not look directly at the perfect orb but saw it slantwise from the corner of her eye. Undisturbed by fog or cloud it met its daily doom and sank. In a few minutes the world grew grey.

While Gerda cooked the enormous asparagus stalks to tender perfection, she made a sauce Hollandaise, wondering if she had lost her skill during the lean unbuttered years. But it was docile to her mastery and turned out thick and unctuous, and yellow as sunlight. Quickly she browned the filet. She lit a candle which she had saved against the failure of electricity. She sat and poured the wine. Then she lifted her glass toward the window and drank.

Slowly she savored the red heart and brown surface of the steak. The asparagus was green as springtime, fragrant as country air. She remembered how it lunged from the dark earth, growing almost visibly. She spread the rich sauce and remembered the churns of her childhood, the long plunging into the darkness and the happy transformation of liquid into solid gold. Each mouthful now transformed her as she felt the happy culmination of her plans.

She thought how well she had managed. It was not easy to come out even. She was smarter than anyone had thought. Miss Helena had never considered her very bright. She had not said so, but some things do not have to be spelled out. Old Mrs. Hopkins had been clearer. There had been a boy from a neighboring farm who had written Gerda after she went to the city to work. He came to visit her. He was a nice boy. But Mrs. Hopkins had looked stern and said, "I feel I must warn you, Gerda. This young person may not have your best interests at heart. He may want just to use you and leave you in the lurch." Gerda knew what was meant. Now after all the years she tasted briefly the bitterness of regret. If only she had known more, earlier. But the disturbing flavor was washed away with the next sips of wine.

Slowly she ate the red berries, alternating each with a mouthful of wine. Red berries, rosé wine. Delicious. Expensive. Wicked. She thought of tomorrow and did not care. She thought of Mrs. Le Grande caught by surprise with all her money unspent. How furious Mrs. Le Grande would be. She laughed aloud and drank another glass of wine. There was a wonderful order in things. One was born, and suffered, and worked. But things turned out. There was nothing to fear. She looked toward the window, which had become very dark. Out there was proof of her wisdom.

She got to her feet slowly. She was floating in a delightful warmth. The room was larger than it used to be. It extended like Bosch's painting. The world expanded. Beyond the shore, the ocean, the horizon, was endless space. She must see it again. But first she must drain the bottle. There must be nothing left.

At the window she could see a bright planet toward the south, and a few specks of stars. These were not enough. She must have it all. She lifted the window and leaned out, but still the view was incomplete. Carefully she climbed down to the sloping roof, and then stood balanced. The sky surrounded her. Stars greeted her. Some wrote her name. She lifted her arm in answer, and the roof tipped. She fell, and rolled into the arms of the air, and kind darkness wrapped itself around her.

At Dan's Place

I never expected to be a waitress at Dan's Place all my life. When my husband got killed I just landed here. And so did the rest of us, sort of. I thought of it one day when Jim Barber had his camera and said, "That was a good feed. You all line up there behind the counter and I'll take your picture." But Dan said he didn't want his picture taken. Mrs. Bybee who helps cook was baking and all over flour. My hair wasn't in too good shape and I didn't feel like smiling at a flash bulb. I don't know if anybody asked Pie Eye. So Jim just snapped Maureen standing by the cash register. When he brought around a print I taped it up by the coffee pot. And now the rest of us is still here but Maureen's gone.

In a little town like this, Dan's Place is a hangout for anybody who has a free hour and wants some company. Besides the regulars we get transients, truck drivers and tourists and salesmen. Nobody ever got sick eating here. Mrs. Bybee's baking is famous clear over to Wanfield. Dan's a nice guy. He keeps old Pie Eye on to help in the kitchen. Pie Eye blew in one day from somewhere, looking hungry. Out front there's Maureen and me. Or was. I don't say we bring in business, but we try to keep it. Nobody likes his plate plunked down by a sour puss.

We had just finished the breakfast rush one Saturday when O'Hare came in looking pretty pleased with himself. He's the trooper on the highway going west out of town. We had already heard about him getting those dope peddlers. Everybody called to him as he swung onto a stool at the counter. Nobody wanted anything but coffee and Danish at that hour, though a P.I.E. trucker was having an Alka Seltzer with his, and Dan came out front too. "Congratulations," he said to O'Hare, "how did you do it?"

"Brains," he said. "Brains and keeping my eyes open."

129

"Just like me," I said. "That's why I'm such a good waitress." We kid around during slack times. Not that there's any rough stuff. Anybody gets too out of line, Dan shows him the door. He's sort of broad, with black hair and a moustache and usually all he has to say is "Get going."

O'Hare turned around on his stool. "Well, I'll tell you. It was really just a hunch. I saw this guy making a full stop at the sign where the side road comes into Highway 2 west of here. It's a place where you can see what's coming away off, and most cars just slow down. It's not legal but it's safe. But this guy made a complete stop and then went on at exactly the speed limit. I remembered him, the way you do. I got to seeing him every little while. He was always just at the legal speed. He never went through the yellow light even. I got to thinking, that fellow is too good to be true. Nobody is that good. So we went on from there and found out he was peddling stuff."

"That was plenty smart. Something to remember in case you want to get by with something," said the trucker.

Mr. Waller, he's in mortgages at the bank, said, "It reminds me when I was in school. When I didn't know the answer I always sat up straight like I was just busting to recite. The teacher never called on me." I took a new look at Mr. Waller.

Mrs. Bybee had come in from the kitchen. "My ma was smarter. She'd say, You look like butter wouldn't melt in your mouth. What you been up to?"

O'Hare paid for his coffee and said, "Give my love to Maureen."

"Sure will. Thanks," said Dan.

Everybody liked Maureen. She worked the evening shift except we both did weekends. She's pretty and as blonde as I am dark. Actually we both help nature out a little. I've been on this job longer than her and I gave her a few tips when she came, but nobody had to tell her how to get along with customers. She just instinctively knows.

She knew how to get along with Dan too. She came in with a load of bus travelers one night. It was raining and she sat on a stool with a scarf on her head. After awhile she took it off and fluffed out her hair, and the whole place lit up. There was a sign in the window, Waitress Wanted. "Is this a good place to work?" she asked me while I wiped off the counter.

"Yeah, especially if you've got six hands," I said.

"How's the boss?" I looked at her. She seemed serious.

"He's a good guy. He's out in the kitchen."

So she got her suitcase off the bus and stayed. We got along fine.

Dan's Place sounds pretty ordinary. It's funny about names. Ones like Sylvester and La Dell may attract more attention, if that's what you want, but there's something about simple ones that sort of inspire confidence because you don't much notice them. They don't jar you. Like Dan Brown. You don't pay any attention to it. My real name is Zenobia. My mother must have been nuts. I keep it dark. People think I'm just Betty. Places like Do Drop Inn and Grecian Grotto and Horatio's Hot Stuff Hideout make me nauseous. I wouldn't ever eat there if I was starving. Enough others feel the same way so Dan does a good business. I and Maureen were efficient and friendly and joked with people, even families jammed in a booth with six kids.

This helped, because Dan is pretty restrained. He's not unfriendly, but once in awhile he seems sort of gloomy, out here where he hasn't any family or anything. He came from the east someplace. "For my health," he said, and that's all. But Maureen cheered him up. She has a cute teasing way with her. After not too long anybody could see Dan was getting stuck on her. No wonder, living alone like he does.

I asked her if there was any question of marriage. "He says he's not the marrying sort," she said. I thought maybe he'd change his mind because he was really getting smitten. I saw them out in the kitchen, leaning against each other like trees in a wind. I don't know what they did when the Place was closed. I tend to my own business.

Dan didn't mind Maureen sort of flirting and horsing around with the customers. It was like the parsley on the edge of a plate, it didn't mean anything. When O'Hare said "Give my love to Maureen" nobody hardly noticed.

Dan's Place isn't where you take anybody on a heavy date but we're always busy on Saturday, and people were still talking about O'Hare getting the dope peddler that evening when I arrived. Maureen was serving a man who comes in once in awhile, but he's not a regular. Usually after a person is here a few times he gets to talking. But not him. He hardly even mentioned the weather in a snow storm. Even Maureen didn't loosen him up. They would talk a few minutes while discussing what was the special of the day, and that was about it. Waiting for her to fill a coffee cup I said, "Do you suppose our silent pal is another of those dope peddlers?"

"He's not the type," she said. "Too standoffish."

I took another look at him. He was pretty well dressed for here, more as if he ought to be at the Belmont dining room. When Maureen set his cup down he said something but neither of them smiled. But later I noticed he left her a good tip anyway.

When I took the tray out to the kitchen I asked Dan what he thought of the guy. He leaned down to look through the service counter. The man was paying his bill and Maureen gave him change. "Thank you, sir," she said, very brief. He nodded and went out. He was medium height, with medium short hair and a medium dark suit. There was absolutely nothing to notice about him except why he was in Dan's Place when he didn't seem to enjoy it much.

"Do you think he's into dope too?" I asked, watching him get in his medium shade blue Buick.

"I don't know," said Dan, picking up one of the toothpicks he uses to pin together club sandwiches. He stood jabbing it into a cube of butter, slowly making a row of dots. "I don't know."

Dan's a fairly big man, in the prime of life you might say. Seeing him peeling or chopping something with that big chef's knife, you think what a funny thing for him to be doing. He looks more like he ought to be boss of a lumberyard or captain of a freighter. I asked him once how he happened to own a cafe. "Fate," he said. "Same as you working here." He made it sound pretty grim. I got to thinking about it. Us in this little joint cooking and serving the same meals over and over, except for the daily special. And even that gets repeated. Wednesday is chicken pie. Fish chowder is Friday. Dan and I have both got a kind of dark side to us sometimes. My joking with the customers is like wearing a clean uniform, it's just business.

Maureen's nature is a lot lighter, like her hair. I think that's what attracted Dan. It wasn't so much that she was pretty but she gave you a feeling like there was always going to be a sunny day tomorrow, no matter what. Even that rainy night when she got off the bus, and took off her wet scarf and shook out her hair, she didn't seem dismal. I don't know if people like that are shallow or not. Maybe they're just lucky and haven't had any black spots to look into yet.

Sunday was an ordinary day. Pot roast and apple pie. A mechanic at the garage took me to the late movie and I slept in Monday because Dan's is closed. Tuesday I had my hand on the door when I saw the sign in the window. Waitress Wanted. Dan was in the kitchen stirring pancakes. "How come I'm fired," I said.

"You're not. Maureen's left." You learn when not to say anything in this business. Some people don't want you to even say good morning until they've had two cups of coffee. I stayed on for dinner. If anybody asked where Maureen was I said she'd left. Her picture was gone too.

Sometimes Dan and I used to have a snack together after the Place closed, before Maureen came. That night I said, "Will you make me a grilled cheese?"

"O.K." he said. He fixed two, and we sat back in the kitchen because the lights were out in front.

"What happened?" I asked.

He sat there awhile like he couldn't make up his mind over the menu. "She was having an affair with that man you asked me about."

"Him? She couldn't. She didn't even like the guy."

"She did all right. They'd been seeing each other. He used to come in here to arrange it."

"How did you find out about it?"

"When I saw them at the cash register, not looking at each other, I knew something was up."

"My God. They sure fooled me."

"They were in her room." He said it like it was a jail sentence for life.

We were sitting at the big table made of a butcher's block and he picked up the mallet he uses to pound things with. Tuesday is Swiss steak. He looked at it a minute and then banged down on the table and our sandwiches almost jumped off the plates.

"Dan," I said, "you didn't—"

"Beat him up?" He gave three little bangs on the table. "No. Her neither."

I was relieved but at the same time I was almost disappointed. Some things are so natural that you get a funny feeling when they don't happen, even if you don't want them to. Like in the movies, when the villain starts out to kill somebody, he has to go through with it, unless something stops him. The hero or something. I had a feeling I wanted to know what had stopped Dan. He's bigger than the other man. He must have been furious, being hurt and feeling betrayed and all. He must have wanted to pop him one. Maybe her too, depending on how he'd found them. It happens in the papers all the time. Jilted lover knocks out rival.

Dan was still playing with the mallet. Why hadn't that big arm hit out and smashed the guy? Sure as ice melts it still wanted to. It was shaped for it somehow, as if that was what it had been made for, what it had been used for. I could almost see it being lifted and falling down on something, crushing it and then hanging there trembling. I found I was trembling too, just thinking of it. I got up and put some leftover coffee on to heat.

All night I kept waking up and thinking. Dan's not a coward. I've seen him handle a couple of real toughs. One had a knife. Of course he was taking care of his property then. But Maureen was too, sort of.

I watched him off and on next day. He's been in town maybe ten years and never left it. He never gets any mail so far as I know from any-place else. He never talks about anyplace else. Most people if you ask "Where you from?" just to make conversation, they're all over you. Not Dan. All he ever said was "East coast." That's a lot of territory. Not that I've ever been there. Out west we take it for granted that it's a good place to leave from. There's a lot of reasons for coming out here. Dan came for his health, he said. I guess he found it. Whatever sickness he's cured of, he must not want to risk going back to get it again.

The new waitress is a town girl. La Rue. She does all right. She talks a lot. She asked Pie Eye who washes dishes why he never says anything. He said, "I noticed once a dog gets in a comfortable spot he don't bark, so nobody's going to kick him out of it."

She laughed but I didn't. I thought of him standing there for the rest of his life scrubbing pots in this little town on the edge of nowhere. And Dan making chicken pie every Wednesday. And me serving it and smiling.

A Little Night Music

ChiChi said, "I'll ride in front with Lossy." Piggy and Ermentrude got in the rear seat of the red VW and arranged their feet around the knapsacks. Sitting in shorts, they seemed to be composed mainly of legs and long hair. In no time Lossy had them on the highway, heading toward the lake. ChiChi started singing "Oh what a beautiful morning." After four years of high school closeness their voices fell into an automatic harmony to which ChiChi sometimes added an unanticipated trill or basso absurdity which dissolved them in giggles. As they passed cars, weaving a serpentine trail and occasionally waving out the window, their voices were caught up and lost in the bright Saturday morning air.

When they turned onto the curving lake-bound road they had to slow down. "This may be our last time all together," said Ermentrude.

"Yeah, it's kind of sad," said Piggy.

ChiChi turned around. "I'll still see you after I'm married. I'm not going into a harem or something."

"It won't be the same," said Ermentrude.

"Let's not mope," said Lossy. "We're out to celebrate." She honked at a cow by the roadside. ChiChi stuck her head out the window with a loud mooooo and the cow stared with its mouth dangling a weed.

"That cow looks just like Miss Simpson," said Ermentrude. "She doesn't know what's going on."

"Miss Simpson tried to keep me from graduating, the old bitch," said ChiChi. "But I did anyway."

"You were lucky," said Piggy.

"They just wanted to get rid of you," giggled Ermentrude.

"So what? I graduated." She craned her head at a sign by a farm. RAZBERRIES FOR SALE. PICK YOUR OWN. "Slow down, Lossy," she said.

"What for?" Lossy's foot was on the brake.

"Let's pick some. Go on down by the trees. Here." ChiChi got out and looked around. A few cars were parked back by the farm gate. No one was near but a man and a woman in mid field. "We can get through the fence," she whispered. "You stay in the car, Lossy, in case we have to make a getaway."

"What'll we put them in?" Ermentrude never had any answers.

ChiChi clutched her head in thought. "My bathing cap!"

They crept between the barbed wires and into the dusty field. Grabbing berries and dropping them into the cap and their mouths, they made a heads-low foray down the row, scratching arms and legs and giggling. Looking up, Piggy saw the man and woman approaching, intent on filling a crate of boxes. They were old people, wearing hats, silent and intent on their labor. "Jiggers," Piggy said. She and Ermentrude scurried back but ChiChi sauntered with her hips swinging nonchalantly until she got to the fence. A barb snagged her bare thigh but she hopped into the car without noticing. Lossy took off with a grinding of gravel.

ChiChi passed the cap around and they ate the mashed berries, their mouths and fingers red. "Bonnie and Clyde never had it so good," said Lossy.

When they got out of the car at the row of attached cabins, blood had stained ChiChi's white shorts. Piggy said, "You got the curse?"

"Jesus," ChiChi said, "I'm bleeding."

"You ought to maybe be relieved," said Lossy.

ChiChi stared at her. "I'm not worried about that. This is from my leg, you dope." She wiped at the blood with a tissue. "It's stopped."

"You're lucky, you got the last double," said the proprietor of Lakeside Cabins. The girls waited while ChiChi signed, listening to several men with fishing poles talk about bait. Their wives stood about, hanging on to their tugging children.

"I hate kids," said Ermentrude.

"You get fat afterwards too," said Piggy.

"Jackie Kennedy didn't," ChiChi reminded them.

"Yeah," said Lossy, "but she had cesareans."

They found their cabin and squeezed into bathing suits.

"Last one in's a pig's placenta," yelled Lossy. They ran and tumbled, splashing and squealing and throwing water. Their fingers lost their berry stains.

But when ChiChi took off her cap, she noticed that it was still faintly pink inside. She stood looking into it. "Those were the best berries I ever ate. Why do things you swipe always taste better than ones you have to pay for?"

"They're fresher," said Ermentrude.

"I don't know if they do," said Piggy. "These were kind of dusty."

"Don't be so damned philosophical." said Lossy. "Somebody put some oil on my back."

They glanced at two boys who slowed down to stare at them. Piggy said, "I'd never date a dude with a tattoo on his stomach."

They spread a blanket and lay in the sun, eyes closed and arms and legs gleaming immobile, like four abandoned mummies. Toward evening they dressed and went to the little cafe under the cottonwoods. Cotton tufts had drifted against the foundation.

"I heard Indians used that stuff instead of Kotex," said Piggy.

"Well they couldn't just sit on a pot in a tent," said Ermentrude.

They jammed into a booth and waited. ChiChi started a rhythm with her fork against her water glass and the others joined in. Idly pinging, Ermentrude noticed that in the booth across the aisle were the two old people who had been in the berry field. They were eating fried chicken, slowly chewing and sipping iced tea. "Wouldn't you hate to be old?"

"Augh. My grandmother has arthritis. And veins." Lossy shivered.

The waitress brought their hamburgers and french fries. They carefully spanked a glob of catsup over everything before they ate it.

"She reminds me of old lady Pismer," said Lossy, peering. "God how I hated history."

"Yeah," said ChiChi. "Me too. You know what I ought to do? I ought to go back and tell her a few things. She was always spouting off about consequences. If the Romans hadn't of done this, something else might have happened. How did she know? Who cares about old dead Romans anyhow? And today. If you don't study you won't pass. If you don't do your homework you won't graduate. Well I didn't and I graduated. So there."

"You were lucky," said Piggy.

"I know what you mean," said Lossy. "If you shoplift you'll get caught. If you aren't good you'll get pregnant."

"Or VD," said Ermentrude.

"My grandmother is always going on about how if Eve hadn't eaten the apple nobody would have any problems. She looks at me like I'd done it," said Lossy.

"Consequences," said ChiChi, slightly choking with her mouth full. "You know what?"

"What?" said Ermentrude.

"I think everything's a matter of luck. Or fate, or something."

"Some people have all the luck," said Ermentrude.

"Yeah. Like Suzanne Ticmaster." Piggy poked out her lips in a puff of air. They sat silent, hating Suzanne.

After they paid their bill they walked along the beach in the dusk. By someone's fence they picked four big red flowers and put them in their hair, helping each other tuck them in. Coming back to the cabin they saw the old couple at the end of the little pier that stopped like a thought too pointless to finish. They weren't doing anything, just sitting looking at the water. "Picking raspberries probably pooped them," said Ermentrude.

"Yeah." ChiChi sighed deeply.

"What's the matter, does your sunburn hurt?" asked Piggy.

"Not much. I just wish Park was here." The rest screamed at her. "No fair! You aren't supposed to even think about him! This is our all-girl party before you get married, remember? No men allowed."

"OK," said ChiChi. "I was just thinking if that was Park and me out there we wouldn't just sit staring at nothing."

"You'll have Park all the rest of your life," said Lossy.

"If you don't get divorced," said Piggy.

"Shut up! I'm not going to get divorced."

"OK so you're going to live happy ever after, until you end up like granma and granpa over there, pooped after picking a crate of raspberries," said Ermentrude.

"I just might. We got a good thing going, me and Park."

"When he gets here tomorrow we'll tell him how you mooned all over the place." Ermentrude clasped her arms over her breast in a languishing wiggle.

"Oh all right, so I'll shut up."

They went inside. "There sure isn't much to do here," said Piggy.

"Should we play some bridge?"

Lossy was on her knees rummaging in her knapsack. She got out something wrapped in a sweater. "Guess what?" Holding their attention she slowly uncovered a bottle of rum.

"Whoops! Where did you swipe that?" Piggy smacked her lips.

"Don't ask! You two go over and get some Coke and ice and we'll drink to something, like living happy ever after or something."

Raising their paper cups in a toast, "To us," they discovered that the red flowers in their hair were already drooping, and took them out. "Flowers ought to last forever," said Ermentrude.

"Orchids last a long time," said Piggy. "Suzanne had one at the junior prom."

"Puke on Suzanne," said Lossy.

Sitting cross-legged on one of the double beds, they played a haphazard game, stopping to replenish their cups of dark liquid. After the first few rounds nobody bothered to keep score. When Ermentrude said, "This is a lousy deal, I pass." ChiChi said, "Me too!" and threw her cards in a wide arc toward the hanging electric light. Leaning back, she started singing "Four little girls from school are we," in their own private version.

"Rum makes you feel like you could go on floating forever, and never stop," said Piggy. "Never ever stop."

"Never ever, never ever," chanted ChiChi, and began one of the unpremeditated moanings that they loved the most. Never ever, they throbbed, keeping a rhythm going on one note and then moving to another, up and down, and clapping their hands softly.

They were startled into silence by a knocking on the wall. It was repeated, three heavy taps. ChiChi picked up her sandal and knocked back. "Please young ladies," said a male voice. "You're keeping us awake."

"Keeping us awake," said ChiChi in a deep hollow tone.

"It's very late."

"It's very late."

"You ought to have some consideration for other people."

"Consideration for other people. . ." she tapered off. The other girls were having spasms into the tumbled bedspread.

The voice stopped. When they could control their faces the girls began to sing with new enthusiasm. There were a few more bangs on the wall which ChiChi sharply returned. Without warning, Ermentrude fell

139

asleep in her underpants and bra and Piggy slumped beside her. The two remaining crawled into the other bed. Lossy stared at the light for an uncomprehending moment and then staggered upright and turned it off.

The sun made a dappled gold highway across the lake when the old couple came out of their cabin. They stowed a couple of valises in the car and stared hard at the red Volkswagen parked beside it. The man yawned and said something. The woman shook her head. They walked down to the beach and looked at the water for a few minutes. Then they drove away. The road was monotonous and empty. The car drifted to the left. The woman said something sharply and grabbed the steering wheel to the right. The man's eyes opened and he steadied the car's progress. The woman covered her eyes with her hand for a minute. They had barely missed the car that had rushed toward them around a bend. They did not see it swerve, and falter, and crash into a ditch, where it lay upside down with its wheels spinning like an agonized insect. At the first town they stopped for breakfast, and were drinking coffee when a police ambulance sped by, it's red light blazing.

The four girls slept late in a sprawl of tangled sheets. When they finally yawned themselves awake they were droopy and silent. ChiChi roused herself and put a faded flower in her hair and struck a languorous attitude with her hip slung sideways, but no one responded. "My mouth tastes like a chicken coop," said Ermentrude.

"Mine too," said Piggy.

They put on their damp bathing suits but only Lossy swam much. The rest splashed around a little. It was noon when they went to the cafe for doughnuts and coffee. The woman at the cash register was talking about the accident. A car went off the road. A man was killed. Coming to work she had seen him put in the ambulance. His head was crushed all bloody. She shivered.

"Who was it?" asked ChiChi.

"I don't know. Just a young man."

At Park's funeral ChiChi sat with folded hands. Her face was pink with tears and sunburn. Lossy and Piggy and Ermentrude looked with awe at her composure. She bowed her head at the proper places, not glancing sideways with a grimace or upward with a clowning parody of piety. Her quiet was almost greater proof of the power of death than the preacher's eulogy and prayer.

It was believed evident that Park must have fallen asleep and driven off the road. This happened all the time. The senseless pity of it struck at the heart of all. Why do such things have to happen, people asked each other, looking into the grave, and went home baffled with silence.

Lossy took Piggy and Ermentrude for an unprecedented and almost formal call on ChiChi. All wore skirts for the first time since the funeral. Instead of plopping down on the floor of ChiChi's room they sat on the bed and a bench. ChiChi's face had gone back to normal. "It's nice of you to come." She too was hollowly formal.

Ermentrude made an effort. "You know how we feel. Just awful."

"Why did this have to happen to me," said ChiChi. "For no reason at all. We were going to be so happy. Why?" They had done no homework on this question and were silent. "If only he hadn't dozed at the wheel. If he only hadn't gone to sleep. I keep thinking, if I'd been there to keep him awake he wouldn't have been killed. I could have sung to him."

They nodded and helplessly watched ChiChi striving. A faint sense of something stirred in her, a zygote from the mating of desire and need. But it died before she could make anything of it.

"Like I said," murmured Piggy, "some people are lucky. I guess some aren't."

"Maybe it was fate," said Lossy. They remembered some instruction from the past, something about a dark creature who lurked at their backs like a monitor at an examination.

"Maybe it was." ChiChi closed her eyes and had a strange glimpse of an old woman leaning over something, her face shadowed by a wide-brimmed hat, her hand reaching out for something, perhaps for her.

The Testimony of Mr. Bones

I don't know the exact week or moment when our love died. But one day I realized that I had been living with a corpse. That evening when my husband came home, he looked through me as if I were a ghost. His kiss on my cheek was a dry touch of convention. After dinner I started what turned into a mutual inquisition. We were both relieved to disinter our feelings and since neither of us believed in till death do us part, we separated. When the divorce was granted I felt as I had the year before after I had agreed to an abortion—free but empty.

I walked along the January street kicking the snow with my boots. I felt the cold touch of falling flakes on my mouth, and knew that I must leave before I perished from the cold. Two days later I was on the bus going south, away from the frozen uplands and piñons and into the plains of cottonwoods and cactus. Next day I was in Mexico, still going south.

I drowsed through much of the flat monotonous desert. There were a few lifeless villages. The bus drove over dead dogs on the highway, scattering the vultures that waited for their meal. When we stopped in towns, I drank beer and ate fritos from a plastic bag, and stared back at the children. On the outskirts of Hermosillo we passed a man carrying on his shoulder a small wooden box. He was followed by half a dozen women, one carrying flowers. I watched them diminish as the bus gathered speed.

The country grew less barren. There were green fields, and irrigation ditches where women washed their clothes and hair. There were shallow rivers and flowering trees. A few miles north of Mazatlan we came on an accident. A local bus had swerved to avoid a car in the middle of the road and had gone off into a ditch. One passenger had been killed, and others were running about screaming. Some of them climbed into our bus and two women crowded into the vacant seat beside me, one with a baby and one with a basket of dead chickens. I was pressed between the window and a bulge of hot flesh. Fortunately Mazatlan was not far.

I stayed in my hotel room almost two days, sleeping, eating a snack from a tray, and sleeping. When I emerged from the dark my skirt fitted loosely.

At a sidewalk table on the Olas Altos I ate an enormous breakfast of huevos rancheros and beans. Sun warmed me. Beyond the promenade wall the sea was flat and blue. As I drank the last of my coffee a small shoe shine boy came near. I shook my head. He dove under the table-cloth and came out smiling. Joke: my shoes were canvas. We both laughed and I gave him a peso.

For two days I roamed the town. I bought a straw hat and silver ear-rings. In the nondescript Cathedral a thin Indian girl, barefoot, with a tiny baby slung across her back, bowed her head at confession. A very old woman crept on her knees the length of the central aisle to the altar wearing on her back a scarf: In Hoc Signo. I wondered what sin could have needed expiation by this slowly crawling shade, and was glad to return to the shabby little Plaza and the smells of fruit and tortillas from the vendors' carts. People here were always eating—hunks of melon and papaya, roasted ears of corn dripping with oil, beans and sweet buns and oysters. Musicians practiced as they walked. Girls and boys eyed each other and smiled. Every female between eighteen and forty seemed to be pregnant. Life crowded around me, indiscriminate as the swirling dust from the sweepers' brooms.

But it was too strenuous. I moved to the tourist hotel on the beach north of the city, and settled down to idleness, swimming in the warm sea, and lying in a hammock under the thatched huts. After dinner I sat on the dark beach. Behind me was the steady thump of music from the bar and now and then a scream of feline female pleasure or a masculine shout. When I moved nearer the shore I could hear the silence and the plunge of waves. Beyond the phosphorescent foam at the sea's edge was the black swelling mass of the fecund sea.

My solitary days came to an end when I met Mr. Bones. I saw him first sitting at a small table in the bar, looking out at the ocean and sip-ping a long white drink. At one adjoining table were four American men in bright Mexican embroidered shirts and bright sun and tequila red-dened faces. They were drinking margaritas and talking about fishing.

On the other side was a middle-aged couple drinking from coconut shells with the good manners of matrimonial boredom in public. The flesh of her back bulged over the top of her brassiere. The man bulged over his snakeskin belt. She kept moving the fingers of her left hand and looking at the diamonds. I looked back at Mr. Bones.

He was a thin man, fairly tall probably, at least seventy. He had white hair and a short white beard and he wore a white linen suit. Where everyone else wore clothing that was gay, gaudy, garish, all that impeccable whiteness was striking. I wondered about him as I drank my rum collins. After awhile he rose to go out and when he passed my table, I glanced at him, and he bowed. He looked older when he walked.

Next morning we happened to meet on the narrow stairs going up to breakfast on the balcony that hangs over the sea. The waiters assumed that we were together, and pulled out chairs for us both. "Do you mind?" I asked.

"I am honored," he replied.

He ate only a small slice of pineapple and a boiled egg. "You must think me a glutton," I said, devouring ham and eggs and a big plate of papaya. "But I'm starving."

"It is proper for the young to be hungry."

"I didn't eat dinner last night. I couldn't bear to sit among all these happy people." We drank coffee and looked at the morning-glazed sea.

"There comes a time," he said, "when happiness is not important. The only thing that matters is life. One's own life. When you have a sense of living, it doesn't matter whether you are happy, or whether you are miserable."

We sat watching the gentle waves. Far out, pelicans were dropping to the water. He said there must be a school of fish.

"Do you come often to Mexico?" I asked.

"I come every winter."

"To escape the cold?"

"That is what everyone thinks. I really come to renew my sense of life."

I watched the pelicans falling and splashing. "Perhaps that is why I came too. I have just been divorced, and I feel rather numb."

After breakfast he said, "If you are really lonely, you might permit an old man to show you a few of the sights. There aren't many." If he had had the slightest leer in his eye I would have refused. But he was old, and cool, and gave an effect of brittleness. Like a sand dollar, delicately etched bleached white, that crushes in your hand. And I was indeed lonely.

That morning we drove in a small horse-drawn cart along the promenade that follows the coast. We stopped to watch a Mexican boy waiting to dive into the water that rushed between rocks into a narrow chasm. He waited a long time on the high peak for an audience to gather, and the wave to be just right. When he dove, the onlookers gasped a little, and then laughed with relief when he climbed out of the foam. We stopped to look at the small bay where the fishermen bring in their catch. Vendors were busily scaling, gutting, tying fish together with a bit of palm leaf through the tails. Pelicans and gulls waited and fought on the beach for the tossed out guts and bones. From the sand rose an ancient stench.

Next day we walked through the big block-square Mercado, where one can buy everything anyone could need for living, anything from pots and huaraches to fowls and freesias. We were touched on all sides by buyers and beggars. Little boys demanded to carry my bag for a peso. A woman in rags held out an empty hand, a child at her skirts, another sleeping in a sling at her back, another growing in her belly. By a small pile of garlic on the floor a very old man sat as if asleep. I was bombarded by the raw colors of oranges and mangoes and tomatoes, and the fragrance of pineapples and guavas and strawberries. The stacks of vegetables, the baskets of eggs and shrimps, seemed endless. So did the stench from the counters of meat, where there were unrecognizable slabs and bits of bloody flesh. The head of a steer sat on one, regarding with open mouth the spilled entrails of its relatives or itself. We left the dim coolness and the carnal smells and came out into the heat of Calle Angel Flores, where a puffy beggar sat drowsing against the wall. Flies circled over the scabs on his head.

We took a cab back to the Olas Altas and drank beer at a sidewalk cafe. From the comradeship of shared sights and smells and movements I thought I understood Mr. Bones. "You are right," I said. "One does feel a sense of life here. All this swarming. The pregnant women. The abundance of fruits and flowers, and the bright crude colors. Even with all the poverty, and the dirt, and the germs, life does go on. And people laugh and sing and make love."

"I am right, but not for the reasons you think." Mr. Bones' silences were cool as a tomb. When he finally spoke again he did not look at me. "There are two ways of continuing to experience things. One is by piling on more and more of the same thing, until one can pile no more. The glutton does this, and the drunkard, and the Don Juan. There comes a time when food and drink and sex, and shapes and colors, and the constructs of ideas, and violence and desire, can not be added to. Then one turns to something else. To contrast. I come to Mexico for that."

I felt the prick of paradox. "You said you came to renew your sense of life."

"I do. But not through life. I get my sense of life through death. Don't be surprised. You too have been touched by it. I have seen you look up at the vultures and shiver a little. You have seen the sea birds feeding on fish and the land birds feeding on crickets. You have seen people barely surviving, and hunger is death's neighbor."

"Isn't this what we call morbid?"

"Sometimes. But even the church encourages it. The monks lived with a skull in their cells. Memento mori. From that bony cup they drank of the waters of eternal life and salvation."

"But you don't want salvation. Or do you?"

"I want to be saved from my inabililty to feel." His voice was insistent and a bit querulous. He looked tired.

On the way back to the hotel I told him about a friend of my mother who used to go to funerals. She picked them out of the listing in the newspaper. We had thought she was a ghoul.

"People keep themselves alive on all kinds of diets," he said. "There have been vampires."

"Even cannibals," I agreed.

That afternoon I lay on the beach and sunned myself. I watched the peddlers with their strings of puppets and bright straw hats. I watched frigate birds circling and waves moving in and out. Lulled at last by this mindless movement, I stopped wondering what would happen to me, next week and later, when my flesh had either swollen or shrivelled in the monstrous carelessness of age.

At breakfast next day Mr. Bones said, "I hope I didn't shock you. The young are offended by the thought of death."

"No, but I was curious. How did you happen to—"

"To feel this way. It is a short story, but it does not go well with orange marmalade, even the bitter variety. Drive inland with me and I will tell you, in a setting that will make you understand."

The day was clear and warm, like all the days. Our taxi swerved through the crowded streets, avoiding other cars and bicycles and dogs and pedestrians, but barely. Mr. Bones was too fragile to hang on to. When we were almost into the country we stopped by an open iron gate in a high pink wall. "Here?" asked the driver.

"Yes," said Mr. Bones. I looked at the sign: Panteon. Mr. Bones bowed slightly, and followed me inside.

We were on the edge of a vast cemetery. From the gate, a road stretched between liana trees as far as I could see. Above us was the flat desert sky, and beyond the walls a blurring of dust and palm trees blowing far off. Inside, here, there was no movement but a man carrying an empty bucket. We saw no one else but an old woman in black kneeling before a grave.

In all directions monuments crowded together in a jumbled democracy. Ornate chapels with a tomb inside stood next to toppled crosses and old stones with undecipherable names. Sculpture rose everywhere in varying degrees of hope or ostentation. Even here there had been fashions, statues that had caught the eye or heart and were repeated until they became as banal as the words on the base—a sorrowing female leaning on an urn, Christ on a cross, an angel with a sweet stone smile. There were cherubs and lambs by the hundreds, on the very little graves.

We left the main road and walked slowly among the paths, Mr. Bones in a white suit and I in a white dress and on my head a white lace scarf that is popular with Mazatlan tourists. We fitted in with the place, for the scene was one of blinding whiteness. Marble and granite and stucco glared in the sunlight. Here and there were bits of color in fresh gladiolus and grave markers painted blue or green, but they were few. Most of the tokens were whitened with dust—paper flowers and vases of eternelles and plastic wreaths, that gave an effect of tawdry transience. More convincing of hope and resurrection was the strange emergence from cracks in the stones of lavender impatiens. "They are miracles," I said.

"Life feeds on death," said Mr. Bones. We walked on, reading names—Romero, Sanchez, Avalos, Acosta. I stopped to translate the words on a tomb, and copied them in my notebook: "Aqui Yacen Los Restos de Dna Leonarda T. de Recasens 1890. Excelente y Abnegada madre sus inconsolables hijos Pablo y Rosa y Angela qui horan su pedida, a su memoria consagran este monumento. R.I.P."

148

"It is all so impersonal here," I tried to explain. "So—dead. I would like to feel that there was one real person, one unselfish mother, whose name I know."

"After awhile one feels some kinship," Mr. Bones said calmly. By this time I was quite lost in the overwhelming chaos of all this decay and dusty grandeur, but he seemed quite at home. He led me to a low wall where there was shade. I sat down and was surprised to hear the cooing of doves. Mr. Bones did not seem to notice. "It would not be the same for you as for me," he said.

"This place?"

"This place. You haven't lived here, as I have. This is the contrast I spoke of yesterday. It is my native land. And this is interesting, because for many years I was afraid of death. When I was a child I wouldn't touch my dead kitten. I wouldn't look at my grandfather in his coffin. I never went to funerals."

"When did you change?"

His silences were too long. "When my wife died twenty years ago."

"So," I thought. "Love conquers all. This fits in with the forlorn hopes on the tombstones."

"What you are probably thinking is not what happened. I was never much interested in women. I married because it seemed the conventional thing to do. I was an accountant and a successful one. I made a good deal of money and I enjoyed my profession. Adding up columns of figures was my life. I thought of my clients as totals on a balance sheet or an income tax return. Of my wife I thought very seldom. She was ten years younger than I, and when she reached the age when women feel their physical charm is going, she ran away with another man. He was the gardener. Perhaps you can imagine my disgust. For a few days I had conventional phantasies of killing her lover, and her. But I knew I would not do it, even to consolidate my honor. I wrote the affair off like a bad account. After a few months she came back. I opened the door and saw her standing under the porch light looking at me. When I closed the door she must have heard me turn the lock.

"Two days later she jumped from a bridge. The police called me to identify the body. When they removed the sheet that covered her I had to force myself to look. I was sickened by the sight. All that had held the face together, to make it the woman I had known, was gone. The muscles had stopped their control. The brain had ceased to care how the face

149

looked. The desire to please was gone. All that was left was a piece of flesh. But I recognized it. Yes, I said, it is my wife. And I went home and vomited.

"I vomited what was in my stomach and then I tried to get rid of what was in my mind. It came up as a bitter green slime. When I rinsed my mouth I saw myself in the mirror and could not believe what I saw. I looked white as a skull and inhuman as a piece of paper. Nothing at all was written on my face—no hate, no love, no greed, no lust. There was not even any wrinkle of curiosity or concern. And I wondered if this was the way I had looked at her when she came to the door that last evening. All night I thought of our two faces, hers battered by life and death, and mine marked by nothing. I thought of this while I arranged for the funeral. Before the service I went to the alcove where the coffin waited. They had performed the usual cosmetic acts, and she was again presentable. I made myself stand and stare at her, and remembered the misshapen grey face in the morgue. Without thinking, I bent and kissed her pale pink mouth. It was the most passionate kiss I ever gave her. Then with the feel of death on my lips I listened to the preacher talking of everlasting life."

His quiet voice had not stopped since the beginning. When I heard the final familiar words I realized I had listened with my head bowed under my white scarf, like a communicant. I raised my head and again I heard the doves cooing, a warm throbbing in the hot air. But I felt cold. There was nothing to say. Our silence was as conclusive as the grave.

Mr. Bones was stiff when he rose. I glanced at him and saw his teeth bared in a grimace of effort and his eyes cavernous in shade under his hat. We walked slowly back to the entrance, past the crosses and Madonnas with Child and the nameless slabs. Fortunately the taxi had returned for us.

At the hotel I thanked Mr. Bones for his story and he thanked me for my company. I turned back to him to ask, "Do you feel fuller of life now, after this morning?"

"Yes," he said, "though you did distract me a little." His gallantry was unfailing.

I pulled off my shoes and my lace scarf and walked along the beach. I could not decide about him. Was he in search of life, as he thought, or was he really revelling in a depraved anticipation of the grave? Macabre indeed. That ghastly kiss must have wedded him forever to the dead.

And yet—I did not know. Afraid of death, he had been deadly. When he embraced it, had he at last been able to feel, had a sense of life and loss burst from him like the impatiens from the stone? Coming so late it had been fragile, and able to bloom only in a place of graves. He could feel his life only by looking at the sepulchres of others. This was his story. Finis.

I stayed awhile longer on the beach, fasting except for an orange I bought from a peddler. I thought of the graves we had passed, of Santiago, Ibarra, de la Pena. Mother's sons all of them, consequence of an inconsequential act. I thought of Donna Leonarda who had unselfishly given birth to Pablo and Rosa and Angela. Here today and gone tomorrow. Mr. Bones too. And I.

I stayed on the beach till sunset. Clouds formed in the west, pale pink, then bright, like the roseate birds on the inland lagoon. Gradually they filled the sky. Carpe diem, I said. This day and all others.

Next morning while I packed my bags I wondered what I would say to Mr. Bones. But a boy brought a goodby message from him: he was indisposed, and wished me a pleasant journey. I sent a note back, hoping for a speedy recovery and thanking him for his kindness. Through the envelope I speared a pink hibiscus.

About the Author

OLIVE GHISELIN says of herself, "From California where I was born, to Utah where I have largely lived, in Mexico and Europe where I have sojourned, I have been a loiterer on the edge of the action." She has taught at the University of Utah and has been writing stories for more than 30 years. Her stories have appeared in publications such as the *Kenyon Review, Michigan Quarterly Review, Quarterly West, The Sewanee Review, Travel & Leisure, Utah Holiday,* and *Western Humanities Review.* She is married to poet Brewster Ghiselin, and this book marks the first publication of her collected stories.

About the Book

THE TESTIMONY OF MR. BONES has been composed by Copygraphics, Inc., Santa Fe, New Mexico, in Garamond #3. The book has been Smyth sewn and printed on acid-free paper by Thomson-Shore, Inc., Dexter, Michigan. The cover is a reproduction of a watercolor created especially for this edition by artist Robert Harvey. Mr. Harvey lives in a village outside of Malaga, Spain, and has exhibited his work throughout the United States and in Europe, Latin America, and Africa.

Teal Press Poetry Series

From the Window, Elizabeth Knies
$7.00, 6 × 9 paper, 64 pages
ISBN 0-913793-02-7

Workbook, Christopher Merrill
$7.00, 6 × 9 paper, 64 pages
ISBN 0-913793-09-4

Fevers & Tides, Christopher Merrill
$7.00, 6 × 9 paper, 64 pages
ISBN 0-913793-10-8

What We Have To Live With, Marilyn Krysl
$7.00, 6 × 9 paper, 64 pages
ISBN 0-913793-12-4

For a catalog of the Teal Press Poetry Series and other titles from Teal Press, write to: Teal Press, P.O. Box 4098, Santa Fe, New Mexico 87502-4098

Teal Press books are sewn for binding durability and printed on acid-free paper for longevity

THE TESTIMONY OF MR. BONES
Stories by Olive Ghiselin

"I love the Western flavor, but the truth is these stories make all life seem exotic. Harriet Doerr and Isak Dinesen come to mind, but there is the brimming life of Lawrence stories and Kipling's India stories, too. The plot often seems at first so neat as to be almost flippant; then you realize the plot is not the story. They raise subtle questions under that enchanting surface."

—*Peter Taylor*

"These stories are as tart and sharp as medicinal herbs. Mrs. Ghiselin has an observant eye, a wry ironic wit, and an unsentimental judgment. But she is no belittler. She can see the human decency in a stodgy Midwestern matron as quickly as she spots the pretension in a phony. And she does not make easy answers. What answer *is* there to the kinds of dilemma that Mary Manfield encounters? What explanation, other than the sort of phony explanation Irving Bott gives the cop, can there be for the humanly curious, harmless, but unorthodox interests of a loiterer? Easy answers appease the easy minded; dilemmas and ironic acceptance are more Mrs. Ghiselin's style."

—*Wallace Stegner*

TEAL PRESS
P.O. Box 4098
Santa Fe, New Mexico
87502-4098

$10.00

ISBN 0-913793-11-6